The Cri...

KEN BRUEN and
JASON STARR!

AUG 2 7 2008

"Two of the crime fiction world's brightest talents, Ken

W9-COJ-702

When they brought Angela to the prison in Lesbos her first thought was, Jaysus, this place lives up to its name. The holding cell held eight other women. Most of them were in micro-minis, skimpy tube tops, a couple even in bikinis. Most were talking in Greek, and a couple of blondes were talking in some other language, maybe Swedish.

Angela went up to one of the blondes, asked, "So is this a prison or a nightclub?"

Thought she was making a joke, but the blonde said, "Both. There was a raid at Niko's last night. Heroin or something. But we have nothing to do with it."

She sounded a little too defensive. Angela glanced down, noticed the track marks on her skinny arms.

"So what did they charge you with?"

"We do not know. They told us nothing."

"What about you?" the other blonde asked. "What did you do?"

"Oh, nothing," Angela said. "I was just having a drink, minding my own business, and next thing I knew two cops were taking me away."

The officers who'd arrested Angela hadn't notified her of any charges. But, of course, Angela knew why she was being taken away. She didn't know if they'd found some evidence that could hang her or if she was just a suspect by default. Not that it mattered. She'd heard enough stories over the years about the Greek justice system. It was your classic, old-world, eye-for-an-eye, guilty-until-proven-innocent mentality. She figured she'd never be formally charged with anything. She'd be handed over to Georgios' relatives and quietly killed.

"Do any of the guards here speak English?" Angela asked.

"There was a young guy here last night maybe nineteen years old. He was hitting on all the women. He told one girl, if she give him blowjob she can get out."

Angela thought, Bingo...

The MAX

by **Ken Bruen**
and **Jason Starr**

A HARD CASE CRIME NOVEL

A HARD CASE CRIME BOOK
(HCC-047)
September 2008

Published by

Dorchester Publishing Co., Inc.
200 Madison Avenue
New York, NY 10016

in collaboration with Winterfall LLC

*This book is a work of fiction. Names, characters, places, and
incidents either are the products of the author's imagination or
are used fictitiously, and any resemblance to actual events or
persons, living or dead, is entirely coincidental.*

ISBN 0-8439-5966-5
ISBN-13 978-0-8439-5966-6

Cover design by Cooley Design Lab

Typeset by Swordsmith Productions

The name "Hard Case Crime" and the Hard Case Crime logo
are trademarks of Winterfall LLC. Hard Case Crime books are
selected and edited by Charles Ardai.

Printed in the United States of America

Visit us on the web at www.HardCaseCrime.com

For Jerry Rodriguez, Megan Abbott and Alison Gaylin

Madison Rules

One

*"I had no worries about someone fucking me. I was no
white bread white boy. If someone said something wrong,
my challenge would be quick and if the apology was
less than swift, I would attack forthwith."*
EDWARD BUNKER, *Education of a Felon: A Memoir*

"Gonna have yer sweet white ass later."

The greeting Max Fisher got from his towering black
cellmate, Rufus.

Max thought, Whoa, hold the phones, there's gotta
be some mistake. Was he in the right place? Where
was the V.I.P. treatment? Where was Martha Fucking
Stewart? Where were those bastards from Enron? How
come there wasn't a goddamn tennis court in sight?
Yeah, Max knew Attica wasn't Club Fed, but he didn't
expect *this*. He thought a big-time player like himself
would get the, you know, special treatment but, Jesus,
not this kind of special treatment. He thought he'd
work on his backhand, get some stock tips, learn how
to crochet, maybe start working out, lose some of the
extra forty pounds he'd been lugging around. Maybe
the guard took him to the wrong part of the prison.
Didn't prisons have neighborhoods just like cities?
Max was supposed to be on the Upper East Side, but

by accident they'd brought him to the goddamn South Bronx.

Max clutched the bars, said to the guard, a young black guy, "Hey, come back here, yo." Yeah, Max spoke hip-hop, one of his many talents. The guard didn't stop and Max shouted, "Hey, asshole, I think there's been a little fucking screw-up around here!" Yeah, let the fuck know who was boss, like the time he was dining at Le Cirque and the maitre d' sat him at a table with a dirty tablecloth. Max let that motherfucker have it all right.

The guard, walking away, laughed, said, "Naw, I think there's gonna be a *big* screw up, Fisher. Inside yo' ass."

His laughter echoed in the corridor until a gate slammed. That's when it finally hit Max—he was fucked. Up till that point he'd been living the high life, in every sense of the word, blitzed from morning till night. He'd once been a highly successful businessman, then he'd had his nagging wife murdered by a psycho mick and things had gone south faster than you could shout *bust*. But rising if not from the ashes exactly, he'd re-invented himself as a dope dealer, and not only that, a goddamn *Scarface*. It didn't last very long, though. He enlisted Kyle, a young hick from way down south, and to say the kid got, um, screwed is to put it very politely.

Throughout his more than colorful career, Max had been haunted, okay *plagued*, by an Irish-Greek woman named Angela, AKA heat on heels. She twice fucked up

his life and twice walked clean away. He blamed her
for his current situation as he blamed her for all his
fucking misfortunes. And yet, fuckit, he still got a
hard-on when he thought about her. But, Jeez, a hard-
on was one thing he did not wanna see right now, in
this cage with Rufus.

Scared shitless, Max looked up to God, or at least
toward the fucking ceiling, and asked, "Why me?"
Yeah, he'd been found guilty of dealing and the judge
had thrown the book at him, calling him a, what the fuck
was the term? Oh, yeah, "a scourge of our society." But
Max didn't think the judge had really, like, *meant* it.
During the trial, etcetera, Max had been so out of it
on dope, he'd thought he was some kind of rock star,
waving to the crowds, and he expected to be found
innocent. Yeah, they were some seriously good drugs.
Finally out of the haze of the drugs, the booze gone
from his system, Max realized he was actually *going to
the freaking slammer*. He screamed at his lawyer, "Get
me out of this, I don't care what it costs!"

His lawyer had actually smiled, the bollix smiled!
Yeah, *bollix*—Max's speech was littered with Irish-isms
from all the mad deranged micks he'd encountered
the past couple of years.

The lawyer had said, "Maxie, you're broke. You've
got like zilch, nada."

Max got the picture, but...*Maxie?* The fuck was with
that? *Dios Mio*. See, he still had his flair for languages,
even spoke spic after his time dealing dope to a crew
of *Columbanos*.

His lawyer had said to him, "Keep your head down."

He'd be keeping his head down all right, on Rufus, it seemed. He'd heard they ran a train through new fish and this was not a train you wanted to board, as it involved lots of guys and your ass.

The reality of the situation had sunk in when the verdict came down but, as he so often did, he'd managed to look at the bright side. Hey, what could you say, he was a positive thinker, an optimistic dude. Maybe this was a reflection of his spiritual training. Yeah, he was a Buddhist, knew how to get into himself, and knew how to not let the negativity of the physical world affect him. He'd asked himself, as he often did during times when his life went to shit, What would Gandhi do in a situation like this? He wouldn't be panicking, that was for damn sure. He'd be getting off on it, acting like, Yeah, a harsh jail sentence, it was a bump in the road, they can beat me up but they can't keep me down.

Like that.

So he'd kept on smoking rock—yeah, he was hooked, so the fuck what?—right up until the day he was due to report to prison, thinking how bad could it be at Attica anyway? Hell, Pacino'd wanted to go there, right? The M.A.X.—that was his dealing name—was a big-time criminal and every famous crime guy had to take a few falls. Look at Dillinger, look at Sutton, look at Capone. It was just part of what you signed up for when you wanted to be the Kingpin, the Big Boss.

As a successful businessman, Max knew that you always had to stay one step ahead of the competition, so to bone up for jail, Max had stocked up on books and DVDs. He'd been given a surveillance bracelet and couldn't leave his apartment, so what the fuck else was he gonna do? He hadn't read anything other than the *Wall Street Journal* since he was in goddamn high school and, let's face it, he didn't read the *Journal*, he just liked to hold it up and stare at it intensely for show, to make people think he was one serious dude who knew his shit. But now he'd started reading for real. The first book: *Animal Factory*. Edward Bunker, now there was one tough mo' fo'. Then he checked out Genet's prison journals till he shouted, "Hold the goddamn phones, this guy is, like, a *pillow biter?*" The fuck with that. But *Stone City* by Mitchell Smith, yeah, he liked the hero in that, felt he might take that road himself. Same deal with *Green River Rising*, Tim Willocks; an innocent guy, caught in a prison riot and, against all the odds, coming out on top. Max could see himself, with true *cojones*, and of course, total modesty, saving captured hostages, offing the really serious psychos and leading the saved out of the burning prison with CNN capturing it all on live TV.

There was also G.M. Ford's novel where Frank Corso had to go into the joint and go up against the meanest muthahs this side of the Mississippi. And, of course, the one by that Keith Ablow dude. Yeah, all the Grey Goose he'd been drinking had put Max at the center of all these novels and somewhere in there he'd realized, prison was *part of his karma*, just one more step in the whole, ok, let's not be shy, messianic road of Max Fisher.

He'd watched Ed Norton in *The 25ᵗʰ Hour* and man, he'd wept buckets. They were like spiritual brothers. But fuck, he wasn't letting anyone beat the shit out of his face, no way Jose. The M.A.X. knew his face was his real ace. *The Birdman Of Alcatraz*? Didn't get it. Never once occurred to him he might be, um, *sharing*. Max had been *El Hombre*, had like over thirty people working for him—okay, only three, including his chef and live-in ho, but who's counting?—and he'd tell his employees not brashly, "Let's get one thing straight. The boss distributes, but share, uh–uh, that don't happen." Feeling like Alec Baldwin in *Glengarry Glen Ross*.

When he'd finished all this reading, he'd been flushed with elation. Whoever played Max in the movie, he'd be a shoo-in for an Oscar. Slam dunk. And, fuck, these books didn't look like they were so hard to write. You could probably just hire some schmuck to write them for you. Isn't that what that guy Patterson did? But it wouldn't be James Patterson "with" Max Fisher—no way that asshole was getting top bill—it would be Fisher *with* fucking Patterson.

Finally Max had had just forty-eight hours left to, like, get his shit together, put his affairs in order and, fuck, get ready to spend the next half of his life behind bars. *Behind bars*. The M.A.X. *caged*? Another book

Max had read: *I Know Why the Caged Bird Sings*. He got halfway through that one before he realized it wasn't a fucking prison novel.

Max had been renting his penthouse—and he was behind on the rent—no problem there—when you go away, go away *owing*. He had the phone cut off and all the utilities, but arranged that they be shut down the day he went to the slammer, so he could have his last forty-eight hours in comfort. He was drinking, not like he used to, but putting it away, Grey Goose, a decent brand, Max still had his taste and sensibility. He was also doing some rock, to keep the party balanced. Probably in the nick, as the Brits called it, he'd have a hard time scoring coke or even crack and he'd have to make do with that homemade hooch they brewed from potatoes. Or, get this, he might attend A.A. in the joint, run those meetings on a proper business footing, give them a little of the Max Fisher class. He tried to imagine himself in the actual joint, saw himself sitting on the floor like some suffering monk. Hell, maybe they'd start calling him The M.O.N.K. Yeah, spending his days in quiet meditation, giving out little pearls of Zen, nuggets of compassionate wisdom to the other inmates. Maybe he'd shave his head, look more spiritual. Fuck, why hadn't he thought of that sooner? Thanks, rock.

On the morning of his last full day of freedom, while taking a morning dump, he stared at his monogrammed towels. He hated to leave them behind but maybe the new tenants, they'd realize they were literally being given a slice of infamy. His reflection, drug induced, showed the eyes of a real caring man, sad but, like, knowing. His face had changed, even he could see that. It was an almost Thomas Merton look, if he could remember who the fuck Merton was. He remembered reading something about Merton living in a sparse cell, writing his seven-story some-shit-or-other. Wasn't he a monk who'd been, like, hotwired in Bangkok? The fuck was he doing there and messing round with electric fires, wasn't it, like, hot enough there?

Max took out the electric razor, raised it, the buzz of it making him jump. Fuck, how loud was the freaking thing? But, nope, couldn't do it. He looked at that gorgeous hair—actually just some thin gray strands surrounding a widening bald spot, but the rock was now seriously lying to him.

With resignation, he said, "It would be a desecration."

He was getting some good wood going and figured he better get that taken care of; wasn't likely to be much, um, nookie in the joint, definitely not of the female kind. A tear trickled down Max's cheek. Fuck, The M.A.X. had been hurt enough, thank you very much. He was going to have a ball during these forty-eight hours and not let them negative waves come at him.

He called an escort service, arranged for two black ladies to come round. He still had about two thousand bucks in bills that not even his shyster lawyer knew about.

So he drank off the Goose, said, "Let's go for bust, baby. Bring it on."

To prepare for the hookers, Max had popped five Viagras and used a pump to enlarge his dick to its maximum three and a half inches.

Then his doorman buzzed, said, "A lady's here to see you."

Lady, in a knowing way, like he was suddenly Mr. Noble. Once Max had asked him for a movie recommendation and the bollix had suggested *Big Wet Asses 2*.

Max knew how to deal with the *help*, and he said, no *ordered,* "Send the fucking lady up and now, and you better watch your attitude 'cause there are, like, you know how many spics crossing the border right now who'd kill for your job? So you know, fella, *get with the game*."

Slammed the receiver, let him know, you fuck with The M.A.X. you better be packing, and it sent him into a flashback of the wild ride of his drug baron days, and him shooting off a whole round at this big black dude who was *shooting at him*, you believe it? The guy had gone down, The M.A.X. had taken him out, taken him *down*, he'd iced that muthafucka, sent him to the big hood in the sky, and the rush! He remembered the kid, Kyle, looking at him, stunned. God, he was so ready now, his wood solid, he'd shoot if the babe didn't get up there in like—what was it that mad mick used to say?—yeah, jig time.

The bell rang and he checked his reflection. The Goose lied large, why you drank the shite, and he saw a suave, ok, debonair, laid-back guy, handsome in the Sean Penn way. You know, dangerous but sensitive too. Splashed on some Paco Rabanne, rapped:

*"Dude smellin' good
Dude smellin' score."*

Opened the door, but the fuck was this? He'd ordered two, right? And didn't booze like, make you see double? Nope, there was one, count 'em, one babe standing there. And *one not so hot-looking babe.* Let's be up front up, one *middle-aged* babe. Had he been watching too much Nick at Night or did she look just like the housekeeper from *The Jeffersons*?

He stammered, "The fuck is this?"

She brushed past him, yeah, you believe it, walked right in, brash as she liked, looked around, what, checking out the pad and if it wasn't up to expectations? Like she would what, leave?

She turned, said, "Y'all Marc Fisher right?"

Marc?

And before he could throw her old ass right out she said the magic words:

"Y'all wanna do some candy first? Yo' down baby, get high with momma, then let momma take care of yo' major action, you really carrying a pistol there, lover."

For a moment Max was tempted to call the escort service, complain, but fuck, he'd maxed out his credit card; it was either fuck the old broad or not get any for maybe ever.

So they did a couple lines, then got to it. Jesus, couldn't she even have a rack? He'd even take an old saggy rack like his ex-wife's, but this chick didn't even have A cups. It was like they were freakin' A minuses.

Max, lost in the coke high, was trying to blow into one of the hooker's nipples, like it was a balloon.

She looked down at him, went, "The fuck you doin'?"

"Er, um, nothing," Max grumbled, realizing he had bigger problems, major *major* fucking problems. Where was his goddamn hard-on? He'd taken how many Viagras and the sons of bitches wore off already?

"Ah, c'mon, you gotta be kiddin' me, Jesus H."

He popped a few more blues, then hopped back on. Still no liftoff and, shit, his heart was racing. Wasn't there a warning about Viagra for heart patients? Was this how he was gonna check out, on top of a flat-chested hooker who looked like The Jeffersons' maid on his last night before heading to Attica? Would that be fucking humiliating or what? What would people think of him? He had a reputation, shit, a *legacy* to protect.

After about forty minutes, Max was covered in sweat and the hooker said, "Time's up, suga," and less than a minute later she left, and Max's last chance for straight sex had left with her.

Now, in the cell, the giant was saying, "You deaf, white bread?"

Max tried to focus, said, "I'm sorry, I missed that?"

The big dude roared with merriment, like he loved this fat, white, balding, middle-aged white man already, repeated, "I got me the top bunk, you got the bottom. You hip to that, my man?"

Max was hip to it, nodded miserably, and Rufus said, "And y'all being sorry, y'all be even sorrier in the morning after I ream yer fat ass, and don't y'all be getting on my case about them condoms and shit. Y'all get the meat raw, know what I'm sayin'? Y'all ain't Jewish or nuttin."

Actually, Max *was* Jewish, but he worried it was a trick question. If he said he was a Jew maybe that would, like, turn Rufus on.

Then Max thought, Wait, didn't all these black dudes convert to Islam, change their names to Mohammed when they got sent away? Shit, Max would be Moslem if it saved his, well, ass.

"We might as well be on a first name basis," Max said. "You can call me Mohammed. Mohammed Fisher."

Rufus sneered, went, "A Moslem shot my mother."

Shit.

Max needed another way out, tried, "I have herpes."

Rufus brushed past Max, going, "Yo, I been havin' herpes since I was eleven years old." Then he said, "Sweep up this here crib, bitch, that's what you are, you my bitch. You gonna get yo' self all prettied up for yo' Daddy."

The smell of his BO made Max want to throw up but Max's whole body was trembling and little did he know, a miracle was nearly at hand. A miracle that would lead Max on a journey to, yes, enlightenment.

But right there and then, Max resorted to what he did when he was most terrified. He went Brit, muttered, "I'm buggered."

Two

*"She knew ways to make a man fuck her, even if he hated her.
When the time came, she would decide."*
JACK KETCHUM, *Off Season*

Angela Petrakos was one seriously pissed off lady. One more country, one more clusterfuck.

She'd been a New York babe, had hooked up with Max Fisher and a mick-slash-psycho-slash-poet, emphasis on *slash*. No need to dwell on the freaking disaster that had been. She was of Irish-Greek descent, some dynamite blend, and she had the temper of both mixed with what Joyce had called "all the sly cunning of her race," only in her case it was races, plural. Went to Ireland and hello, like, why the hell did nobody tell her those micks had gotten rich and just a tiny bit cute? Not cute in the American sense—no, cute as in manipulative greedy bastards. And she—Jesus on a wobbly bike, would she never learn?—had hooked up with a guy who looked, okay, hot. Dark long hair, cool, though rip-off shades, the dangerous leather jacket, black naturally, and a way with him. He rocked back and forth on his feet, made her feel like she was, yeah, gorgeous.

Cut to the chase and chase it was. They'd had to flee to America and would you believe it, back into a scheme where yet again she tried to make Max Fisher pay for the shite she'd endured.

She sighed at the memory, muttered, "Let it slide."

So she'd grabbed some bucks and gone to Greece. Visited some relatives in Xios, but that got old fast, so she ferried to Santorini, supposed site of Atlantis. Got to be good karma there, right?

Um, for a start, what was with the fucking donkeys having to carry you up the cliff to the town? She must've missed that in the guidebooks. But being American carried some weight still, especially if you were a hot, stacked blonde.

She rented a small villa and was surprised at how cheap it was. Georgios, who owned the place, also claimed he was mayor of the village and drove a cab at night and was the chef at the local taverna. These Greeks, they knew how to multi-task. He was ogling her openly, staring at her bust to the point where she had to hit him with the old "My eyes, they're, like, up here." At the door, he held her arm and reminded her how reasonable that rent was and how, if she was a little cooperative, the rent might disappear completely.

She knew some Greek, about four words but all the vital ones, and said, "Mallakas," i.e. wanker, and he fucked off.

First it was heaven, the balcony overlooking the sea, sipping on some ouzo, her tan coming along nicely, showing off her serious cleavage. The nude beaches were great, but the constant Greeks hitting on her became a drag. She was so desperate she would've settled for a mick.

She was offered a job as a hostess in a club named *"Acribos."* Her second Greek word: "Exactly."

When she wasn't tanning, she was hiking in the dunes, or just hanging out at the local taverna spinning worry beads, drinking ouzo, and playing backgammon. It was relaxing but, let's face it, boring as hell. She was Angela Petrakos. She needed a buzz, she needed action.

She made a friend at the taverna—Alexandra, an American from Berkeley. They decided to hit the clubs one night and a hit they were. It might've helped that they were the only two women in the place without facial hair, but guys were all over them all night. Near closing time they hooked up with a couple of young Italians who claimed they were eighteen but Angela figured that hers, Luca, was sixteen tops. Alexandra and her guy disappeared, and Angela and Luca wandered down to the beach. She had a full moon, crashing waves, and a horny young Italian. What else did a girl need?

And the guy might've been a teenager but, boy, he knew how to screw. They went at it all night till they collapsed in exhaustion. In the morning, Luca was gone and so was Angela's money. The little bastard had gone through her purse and cleaned her out. Good thing Angela wasn't carrying much. The kid got sixteen euro, Angela got six orgasms. Who got the better deal?

Alexandra left town the next day and Angela was back on her own again. People had been getting to know her and generally treated her fine, but this one old woman, must've been a hundred, gave her the heebie-jeebies from day one. When Angela walked along the streets most people would say *yassou*, hello, to her. But this woman would just glare at Angela, giving her the Evil Eye, as if she knew, but knew what?

Then one evening at the taverna, she was beginning to get that bored, pissed off feeling again—never a good sign—when she heard, "My word, what a vision of true beauty."

Turned to see this tall guy, looked like that writer Lee Child, whom she hadn't actually read but from the photos on the back of his books she nearly believed there might be a reason to read those mystery novels. She had a Barry Eisler book cause of his jacket photo and one by C.J. Box—hey, she'd always been a sucker for guys in cowboy hats. Who cared if these guys could write, they looked hot. No wonder the Micks had to actually write books, mangy-looking bastards they were.

The Lee Child guy was wearing, oh saints above, a safari jacket, and he had that young Roger Moore look. The best part: *A British accent.*

She muttered, "Thank you, God."

Finally, her luck had changed, a Brit, was there an American gal on the planet didn't want to hear that *Brideshead Revisited* tone?

He asked, oh those fucking make-you-moist manners, "May I join you?"

She would've let him do a lot more than that. But she figured, British guy, he was probably reserved and well-mannered. She didn't want to turn him off and be, like, too forward.

"Oh, yes, please do," she said, trying to sound British, but the American was coming through loud and clear.

He held her hand, kissed it, said, "I'm Sebastian."

God, that accent! She was tempted to shout "I'm available!" but went with, "I'm Angela."

He told her all about himself. Said he was living off a trust fund, traveling the world, and he was, naturally, writing a novel. The writing part she could've guessed. For some reason, she was a magnet for those literary types—maybe it was a misery-loves-company kind of thing.

When it was her turn she knew honesty was the worst policy. She said she'd lived in New York for a while but things hadn't worked out with her fiancé, then she'd moved to Ireland for a while, tried New York again, and now she was giving Greece a shot. She, er, forgot to mention all the violence.

He looked her in the eyes, held her gaze, and said, "I must say, in all my travels, I've never encountered anyone quite as stunning as you."

An all-too-familiar voice in Angela's head was screaming, *Run! Get the fook out while you still can!* How many times had she been down this road, meeting a guy who seemed like "the one," only to wind up screwed, and not in the good way? She didn't have baggage, she had freakin' cargo. Or, as they say in the south, she'd been *ridden hard and hung up wet*.

Translation: She didn't trust nobody.

Later, when Sebastian asked if he could give her a lift home, Angela said politely, "No, thank you."

She hardly believed it herself. Had she really turned down an easy lay with James Bond's twin?

"I must see you again," he said.

His eyes looked so vulnerable, like Colin Firth's. She was tempted to say, screw it, and drag him back to her place and fuck him stupid. But she remained strong, said, "Well my schedule's pretty full."

"Surely you can squeeze me in somewhere," he said, punning like ol' Roger Moore himself.

But she remained strong— when had she ever had the discipline to do that?—and told him, "Maybe we'll run into each other again sometime."

But he insisted on seeing her and she said she "might" be able to meet him for a drink at a taverna near the beach the next afternoon.

Of course she showed. The following night they went out to dinner. At the end of the night he gave her a peck on the cheek goodnight and asked her when he might have the pleasure of seeing her again. She didn't sleep with him until the fourth date—okay, the third, but who's counting? Still, it had to be some kind of record.

And then one night, not long after, he uttered the lure, the never-fail, hook-'em-every-time words and, even more damning, in Greek: "*Sagapoh.*" I love you.

In any language and especially in that British accent, she was signed, sealed and *kebabed*. It was beautiful, lyrical, her beau had finally arrived. He was even talking about taking her to England for a weekend to meet his Mum and Dad. Yeah, she was seriously getting into the idea of marrying Sebastian, settling down, becoming British. Her grandfather, the Brithating bastard, would probably turn in his grave, but who gave a shite? She'd be like Madonna. She was already refining her accent and when they got married maybe she'd adopt an African child or, hell, steal one.

She felt like her life was finally starting to get on track. She was still young, just thirty-three. Maybe twenty or thirty years from now she'd be happily married to Sebastian, their kids off at University, and she'd laugh at some of the "mistakes" she'd made early on in her life.

One tiny little glitch hardly worth mentioning, but one night, they were dining at a posh restaurant overlooking the seas when the waiter returned with Seb's Visa card, saying it had been refused. But it was no biggie. As he put it, "Nothing to get your knickers in a twist about, love."

Angela paid in cash, tried to pretend she hadn't noticed a glint in Seb's eyes, no, surely a trick of the Greek light. And okay, so she seemed to be picking up the tab more often, and Seb, the handsome rogue, holding his cig exactly like she'd seen in all those movies, saying, "Darling, slight hitch with the old trust fund, they want to increase my allowance but I damn well refused, I'm writing an opus to make Lawrence Durrell want to weep, so I say damn their impertinence, I'll pay my own way or go down like Khartoum, blazing but bloody defiant."

The fuck was he talking about? She didn't care, she loved it because of the accent. And she loved he was an artist, a real writer, not like her old boyfriends, Dillon with his poetry and Slide with the fucking screenplay he kept talking about. So what if she never actually saw Sebastian, um, write? Once she wondered, Wouldn't, like, a laptop have helped? But she refused to give in to those negative waves. She figured he was literary, kept it all in his head. This was love, the real thing; so what if there were a few inconsistencies? As her mick exes used to say, "Damn the begrudgers."

Then one evening she was at her villa, showering, when she heard a noise in the other room. She figured it was Sebastian, as she'd given him a key to her place.

"Come in, Sebs, darling, I'm feeling quite horny at the moment and a bit of a screw in the shower would be lovely indeed."

Yeah, the Madonna accent was coming along well.

She parted the curtain, smiling, expecting to see Sebs, and then gasped when she saw Georgios, her landlord. His squat body, the clumps of hair from out of his dirty wife-beater, that scowling look—he was like some kind of deranged animal. And, fookin A, was that a *meat cleaver* in his hand?

He growled in Greek, spraying saliva, ending with,

"you dirty cunt," and came after her. She managed to duck to her left just in time, the cleaver slicing through the curtain. Naked and wet, she darted out of the bathroom, screaming, but he tackled her from behind. He had the cleaver to her throat.

She closed her eyes, waiting to die and to be with her mother and father again—she just hoped to God there wouldn't be spoons and bodhrans in heaven.

But he wasn't going to kill her, not yet anyway. She should've known.

When he was through, his sweat was dripping, no *pouring,* off his body, onto the back of her neck, and he leaned closer to her, said, "You be my wife, okay? You drive taxi, okay?"

Then she heard, "By God, love, are you all right?"

Sebastian, the useless bastard. He sees her lying on the floor underneath a mad Greek rapist and he asks if she's *all right*? She was tempted to say, Yes, I'm doing wonderful, darling. Why don't you put the kettle on and come join us?

But she noticed that Georgios was momentarily distracted and she seized the opportunity and went for the cleaver. The bastard wouldn't let go of it, so she had to bite on his ear, as hard as she could, tasting the sweat and blood. Meanwhile, out of the corner of her eye, she noticed that Sebastian was just standing there with a curious expression, like he was watching a fookin' snooker match. These Brits, unless they were shooting boyos they were feckin' useless.

Angela didn't stop biting on the Greek's ear. Finally,

after she'd kneed him in the balls a couple of times, the cleaver clanged to the floor and she grabbed it. She started hacking into his chest, slashing and swiping. It seemed like all of the past few years were welling up, fueled by the smell of this fooking animal. And she let him have it, all right. Never fook with a woman who has the Greek-Irish gene.

She was kneeling over her victim, gasping, her hands covered in blood. Then she raised the cleaver again and Sebastian went, "Darling, it's not necessary, the bugger's already done for."

Through her pain and rage, the Brit accent gave her a moment of joy. Then she heard the word *bugger*. By fuck, *bugger*.

Georgios, somehow still alive, was coming round, muttering, "Mallakas, menu…?"

She'd give him mallakas, thinking of all the ferocity she'd learned from the micks in her bedraggled life, all the shite from one Max Fisher who'd once said, "Gonna put the meat to you, bitch."

She'd let the bitch part slide, but *meat*? All three inches of his top sirloin?

She raised the cleaver and Sebastian, in that beautiful accent pleaded, "Darling…don't."

She grabbed Georgios by his hair, gave him one ferocious slash across the neck, nearly decapitating the bastard, then said, "Word to the wise, *darling*, don't ever fuck with me."

Then she and Sebastian were on the floor, going

at it like animals. The power surge, as she saw the majestic Brit underneath her, her *using* him, and saw—was it fear?—in his eyes. Probably had a little to do with the cleaver still grasped in her right hand. What you might term a power ride.

He whimpered, "Darling, this is all quite nice, but is the, um, weapon necessary?"

And she began to laugh, laugh and come, swung the cleaver across the room and it landed with a pleasing thump against the wall.

Later, when she came round, Sebastian had cleaned up, the Brits, a tidy race. Georgios was neatly wrapped in a roll of plastic sheeting and the blood splatter had been washed clean. She wrapped a flokati rug around her and Sebastian, looking like death warmed up, gave her a cup of the thick sweet Greek coffee, and said, "Precious, we might be, um, in a spot of, um, bother."

She nearly started laughing again, said, "Bother. Trust me, lover, bother is my forte."

She drank the coffee, handed him the cup, demanded, not asked, "More." Then ordered, "Put some of that Metaxi in it, I need to focus."

Making it very clear who had the balls in this relationship.

By dawn's early light, they'd used Sebastian's tiny scooter and driven precariously to the cliff on the other side of the island. All the time, Sebastian expecting the cops to stop them at any moment, and them carrying a literal dead weight between them, on a *bicycle built for two*, as that awful song goes. Angela behind, a new Angela to him, urging, "Get a fooking move on, people will be moving soon."

Lord above, she scared the daylights out of him. He'd thought he'd scored himself a rich American dumb blonde and instead had the Greek version of *Fatal Attraction*, with a cleaver no less. Oh lordy, how had he gotten it so wrong?

She was screaming, "What kind of bike is this for a man? You ever hear of a Harley? Like, a *man's* machinery?"

He was too scared to answer, the demented creature had probably still got the cleaver somewhere. She had seemed awfully attached to it and if he lived to be a hundred, scratch that, if he got to see noon, he'd never forget the way she'd hacked the poor Greek bastard to ribbons. And yes, he hadn't been the most useful person in her predicament, seeing the randy chap, um, *having his way with her.* Gosh, it had been almost exciting. And to say she'd overreacted, I mean *really*. Didn't she know those Med types were hot blooded? It wasn't like the gell (pronounced thus) hadn't been down the M1 before. And then, oh lordy, the cleaver. She was like some bloody Irish gutter-snipe.

He'd been in some scrapes, a chap doesn't get to his late twenties, alright, mid-thirties, without the odd ruction, but this, this was like, what was that awful

Hollywood tripe? *Texas Chainsaw Massacre?* This was like living a gosh-awful B-movie he and the chaps might rent after a night on the tiles in Cambridge.

Oh, he swore, by all that Cambridge held sacred, if he got free of this mad cow, he was legging it back to Blighty and scoring some dosh however he might and heading straight for Italy, some civilized European country where being British still counted for something. Naturally Sebastian had never actually been to Cambridge. He'd flunked out of a third-rate technical college but come on, isn't a chap allowed a little *leeway*?

And weak—no one knew better than he how lily-livered he was. As a child, he'd seen the movie *The Four Feathers*; that was him without the end heroics and redemption. He got by on his diminishing trust fund, wonderful manners, sheer culture and, dammit, his boyish good looks. No one, he knew this, no one could do that toss of the black lustrous hair, the vulnerable little-boy-lost look better than he. He had nothing else going for him, he knew that, but with a little luck he'd been hoping it would, at the bloody least, net him one of those rich dumb Americans of which the States seemed to produce a never-ending supply.

She was hammering his back. Damn it all, his back was fragile, old rugger injury. Okay, he never played, but he did follow the game all right.

She was screeching, "Here, you dumb fook."

Crikey, her language was simply appalling.

They dropped ol' Georgios off the cliff and Sebastian, nigh hysterical now, wanted to shout, as the body hit the ocean, *Beware of Greeks bearing cellophane*. And he thought, dammit, he might just yet write the great Brit novel. Evelyn Waugh, eat your bitter heart out.

Three

Hell hath no fury like a mystery writer...dropped.

Paula Segal was nervous, not a feeling she liked having. She laughed to herself, thinking, *Feeling Nervous*, she might use that for a title. Or *Twisted Feelings*? Or maybe *Hard Feelings*—someone else had probably already used that but fuck him, you couldn't copyright a title. Then she sighed and said out loud, "Bad joke." Like she was ever going to have a shot at titling another book.

She was meeting her agent for lunch, not dinner. You knew when they moved you from dinner to lunch, you were semi-fucked, only one unearned-out advance away from a fast latte in Starbucks. Just ask that poor Irish bastard who'd been hot for all of ten minutes. Jesus, he'd had more agents than lattes and look at him now. He couldn't even make a panel at the U.K. Festivals.

She checked her rankings on Amazon—nothing better than 500,000. And worse, she'd gotten yet another shitty review from *Booklist*.

The thing was, she knew she was good. She had three good mysteries under her belt, one nomination for the Barry—she'd lost to Tess Gerritsen, but that was no biggie, everyone lost to Tess—and Laura Lippman had promised her a blurb. Even Val McDermid had smiled at her that time in Toronto.

But she'd been termed "midlist" when she'd started out and more recently had slipped to "cult." Cult equaled nada, sorry, hon. She just didn't get it. She thought only those creepy noir guys got demoted to cult. She'd never even written a short story for Akashic.

She seriously didn't understand why her books hadn't done better. She wrote what she thought was a nice blend of cozy and medium-boiled. Nothing too dark or too scary. Her heroine, McKenna Ford, was a lovely combination of sensitivity and street smarts.

But not according to *Kirkus*, which called her last book, "Tired, unoriginal and pointless. Read Megan Abbott for the real deal."

Jesus, she hated Megan Abbott and Alison Gaylin. Not only did the guys love them but they got rave reviews. Don't get her started on female mystery writers, except for Laura of course. Hey, that blurb might still happen.

Her agent ran her rapidly through lunch, then said, with no gentle breaking in, "You're screwed."

Lunch that.

He added, "SMP's dropping you." Then asked, "You ever try true crime?"

What? She was an artist. She couldn't slum and

write non-fiction. She was going to just say, fuck it, it wasn't for her. If she couldn't write mystery fiction she'd rather go back to the telemarketing cubicle.

But then her agent told her about the Max Fisher story and something sparked. She thought, *Hello?* This could be a goldmine; it was like the book was already written. She couldn't believe Sebastian Junger hadn't beaten her to it. Could The M.A.X. be her ticket all the way to the top? Or, well, at least back to the middle.

As usual, she got ahead of herself. She imagined winning next year's Edgar Award for best true crime book, with her old editor sitting in the audience watching, thinking about the one that got away. Maybe Laura herself would present the award. Though they'd only spoken that one time, at the bar at the Left Coast Crime convention in El Paso, and let's face it, Paula had been so nervous she barely spoke. She just did a lot of smiling, nodding, and blushing. Still, she felt like Laura actually liked her, that they'd, dare she even think it, made a connection that went way beyond mystery writing. The encounter had ignited something in Paula, gotten her off the fence, so to speak. She'd experimented in college—who hadn't?—and a bit after college, too, and yeah, once or twice in recent years, but basically she'd thought of herself as straight. But that smile Laura gave her had pushed her over the edge. Hell, over the cliff. Yep, Paula was playing for the other team now. She was on the lookout for a pretty, intelligent, mature, successful lover and Laura Lippman fit the bill. She imagined them living in Baltimore, their Edgars side by side on the mantel, traveling the festival circuit in Europe together...

Okay, okay, it was time to focus, buckle down, get this damn book written.

She attended the trial of The M.A.X. She sat in the back, taking lots of notes. This Max Fisher, he was some character all right. She'd never seen anyone so caught up in his own delusion. He was on trial for major drug charges, and it was like he was gleefully oblivious to it all. Even when the judge sentenced him, Fisher didn't seem to get the gravity of the situation. As he was led out of the courtroom, he chanted, "Attica, Attica, Attica..."

Paula knew she'd have to dig deep, really make readers understand the psychology of Fisher, but deep wasn't her strong suit. Her writing was surfacey, superficial. She often told friends that this was purposeful, that she could write with more depth any time she wanted, that she consciously tried to "dumb it down for the masses." As if the masses had ever seen one of her books. She had a better chance of bedding Laura Lippman than of getting a book into Wal-Mart.

But a superficial take just wouldn't work for a guy like Fisher, and neither would her usual cozy-to-medium-boiled style. This guy made *In Cold Blood* seem like chick lit. The things the man had done, the unsavory people he'd been involved with, especially

that woman he'd been engaged to, Angela Petrakos—
she sounded like she could be the subject of her own
true crime book. Paula was already thinking, sequel?
But telling the Fisher story properly would require
some serious hardboiled, noir writing. She didn't know
if she had the chops to pull it off.

But the telemarketing cubicle loomed large and
made her refocus. She Googled like a banshee and by
the time she was done she was thinking, *Edgar? Just
the beginning. Why not a National Book Award? Or,
hell, maybe even a Quill…*

She had to sit back and try to take it all in. The Fisher
story had it all. There were, get this, Irish hit men who
even had, whisper, *IRA connections*. There was also
some odd stuff about Down Syndrome and gold pins
that she didn't quite get but hey, if there was a handicapped theme, hello *Oprah*, right? What would she
wear on the show? Would Oprah cry when Paula talked
about her long personal journey from unknown cult
writer to literary goddess? Yeah, probably.

She snapped herself back into focus, thinking, And,
wait, there was even more handicapped stuff, some
guy in a wheelchair who photographed women in, let's
say, compromising positions. Hello *Playboy* serializa-
tion. And there was also

A hero cop: Hello Hollywood. At worst, a TV series.

Boyz in the hood: Hello Spike Lee.

Southern crackers: Hello *National Enquirer*.

And above it all, loomed The M.A.X. There was

no doubt that was the book's title: *The Max*. She'd thought about *Hot Blood, Tough City*, toyed with *Songs of Innocence*. But, nope, it had to be *The Max*.

She was so excited. She went and made herself a dry martini; no one, she knew it, no one, made them drier. It was good, just the right amount of martini, and gave her the boost of confidence she needed as she wrote the following to Mr. Max Fisher, c/o Attica State Penitentiary:

> *Dear Mr. Fisher,*
>
> *I am a mystery writer of high standing in my genre, a friend of Laura Lippman, Tess Gerritsen, etc. I have been commissioned by a very high profile publisher to write a true crime book and I truly feel you are the subject most deserving of my time. I believe you have been the most appalling victim of our Justice System and I would like to set the record straight and I must confess, as a woman, I find you hugely appealing. I enclose a photo.*
>
> *Yours sincerely*
> *Paula Segal (MWA, IACW, ITW, PWA)*

She had the perfect photo for this schmuck—her, bursting out of a bikini, nearly topless. And her favorite part about the photo, she looked demure. Demure was a word you got to use when you were a writer of her caliber. Recalling the photos of Petrakos from the trial, she knew this asshole loved big busts, and was he ever getting the max with this shot. Her previous lover, an Annie Lebowitz wannabe, had taken it. The girl was a lousy lay but she sure could take good photo.

Delighted with her herself, she practically skipped down to the post office and sent the letter. Attica, just the thought of it made her shudder.

Four

"I think you should get on my body now."
DAVID MAMET, *Edmond*

It wasn't like Max had never been raped before. During a drinking binge in the south he somehow wound up in a motel room in Robertsdale, Alabama with a Chinese guy named Bruce. Maybe it wasn't technically rape because Max might've gone up to the room willingly, but really the saving grace was that he'd been so bombed he couldn't remember any of it.

Man, what he would have given for some hard liquor right now.

The worst part, it was only around noon, and he had nine hours till Rufus and lights out. First, lunch in the mess hall. Jesus Christ, eighty percent of the prisoners were goddamn black. He felt like it was that time in the city he was so absorbed reading a copy of *Screw* that he missed his stop on the 6 train and got out at fucking 125th Street. Walking through the mess hall he was thinking, *Be Richard Pryor in Stir Crazy.* He was even whispering to himself, "That's right, I'm bad, I'm bad." But he must've been shaking his ass too much because the walk didn't get him any respect—it had the opposite effect, getting him catcalls from all the guys. They were whistling at him, calling him "sweety" and "honey," and Max, shaking, thought, Jesus Christ there was gonna be a goddamn gangbang.

He knew he had to do something to get some respect. Maybe he should make a shank and cut somebody. Isn't that what that Eddie Bunker said you were supposed to do? Yeah, but how the fuck was he supposed to get a shank his first day in the joint. Eddie, couldn't you've given us a goddamn instruction manual?

Later, in the yard, more guys were eye-fucking him, saying things like, "Gimme some a dat" and "I wanna tap that big ol' ass, gran'pa."

Gran'pa?

That was the part that stung the most. Yeah, Max was in his fifties, but he'd always seen himself as a hip, happening dude. It hit Max that not only was he a lot whiter than these guys, he was a lot older. It seemed like every guy was a goddamn twenty-two-year-old. What, was he the only guy in the world over fifty who was into drugs and shooting people? He had thirty plus years on all these guys, so how come they weren't treating him like the wise elder statesman? How come he wasn't getting respect, like Morgan Freeman in *Shawshank*? Speaking of *Shawshank*, Max wasn't going into the prison laundry room any time soon. Not until he made that shank, anyway.

As much as he feared the inevitable sexual assault, Max had to admit, on some level, all the attention was kind of, well, flattering. He couldn't get women to look at him the way these guys were unless he was paying them good money, and even then Max never felt *liked*. Jesus, it was bringing tears to his eyes. The M.A.X. crying? At *Attica*? Jesus, that had to be the absolute wrong thing to do—show your weakness. But he couldn't help it. Maybe he was channeling his inner sissy, but what could he say? It felt good to be wanted.

A guy in the yard was bench-pressing—he looked Mexican, Puerto Rican, Dominican, something Spanish Harlemy. And the son of a bitch was huge, looked like he could be a linebacker for the fucking Jets.

Benching what looked like at least three hundred pounds he said, *"Hola, jovensita,"* and blew Max a kiss.

The M.A.X. knew his Spanish, the guy was calling him "young lady." *Jesus H.*

Max turned away and the guy said, "Hey, I finish talkin' to you, *mi puta*?"

Max tried, *"No hablo español."*

"Don't worry," the guy said, "you don't gotta talk *español*. When you got my dick in your mouth all day I ain't gonna hear nothin' you sayin' anyway."

The guy laughed then let the weight fall onto the brackets so hard the whole bench shook.

"Look," Max said. *"No necesito* trouble." Then, hearing the hillbilly in *Deliverance* saying, *You in trouble now, boy*, he said desperately, "I mean, I've got *nada* against Puerto Ricans."

"Puerto Rican?" The guy sounded offended. "I look

PR to you? Man, I should cut you just for saying that shit. I'm fuckin' Panamanian."

Jesus, weren't Panamanians supposed to be, like, midgets? The only fucking Panamanian giant on the planet and Max had to run into him. Was that shit luck or what?

Then the guy said, "I should introduce myself properly, if you're gonna be my little *puta*. *Me nombre es* Sino."

Sino? What was that, fucking Chinese? The guy wasn't fucking part Chinese, was he, some kind of ChinoManian? Max had had enough Chinamen visit his ass for one lifetime, thank you very much.

"Sino's what they call me in the Bronx, shit's short for *asesino*. You know why I got that name? 'Cause I like to kill people, that's why. I killed sixteen people and you gimme your ass you won't be number *diecisiete*. Most people in here, they don't like to talk about people they took out, think it's gonna fuck up their parole. But Sino got Life, No Parole hangin' over his ass. Sino ain't goin nowhere so Sino don't give a shit."

Max was about to give a shit—in his pants. But out of nowhere Rufus appeared and said, "Yo, lay off my bitch, *bitch*, 'fore I beat yo' ass."

Sino stood face to face with Rufus, both mad bastards about the same height, and a crowd formed around them to watch the confrontation. Max felt like he was in high school—well, not like he *himself* had felt in high school, but like he might've felt if he'd been a popular girl in high school. It was like Max was head cheerleader and the two jocks were fighting over him. Max had to admit—it felt pretty damn good.

But the good feeling passed quickly. Max was thinking maybe he should've taken the Ed Norton in *The 25th Hour* route after all, gotten somebody to beat the crap out of him before he went away. He was just too damn pretty. A face like his, naturally guys couldn't resist it. Maybe if he hadn't been so interested in getting laid during his last forty-eight hours, and hadn't wasted all his time reading books and watching movies, he could've thought of this practical shit.

Rufus was yelling into Sino's face, "Mohammed Fisher's my bitch. Stay off my bitch, know what I'm sayin', bitch?"

And Sino was screaming back: "I don't see no sign on his ass say he your bitch. I don't see your dick in his ass neither."

Rufus said, "There don't gotta be no dick in his ass. Just 'cause there ain't no dick in his ass don't mean the bitch ain't mine."

Max was tempted to yell, *You're both fucking morons!* but had a feeling that wouldn't go over well. Maybe the guys would decide to share him, holy fuckin' shit.

A guard came over and told the guys to break it up. Rufus grabbed Max by the hand and led him away.

Later on, back in their cell, Rufus said to Max, "You clean yo' ass out good tonight, know what I'm sayin'? I don't want no brown on my dick. My dick got enough brown on it, don't need no more, know what I'm sayin'?"

There was nothing for Max to do now but lie in his bunk and wait for the inevitable. He was thinking about, of all people, Elvis. Max, in those last forty-eight hours of freedom, had watched so many movies, his fucking eyes hurt and how he ended up with *Jailhouse Rock* in his DVD player was anyone's guess. The King, singing on the tiers, had brought tears to his eyes. He'd never really given Elvis a whole lotta time. Let's face it, The Max was a classical music kinda guy, could pronounce Tchaikovsky without a single moment of hesitation. *Fucking hum that, yah morons.*

Shit, he realized he'd been talking aloud again.

"Well, fucking excuse me!" he shouted. "I'm under a little goddamn pressure here!"

Inmates in the other cells starting laughing and Max blocked it out, thinking about Elvis again. The El was one good looking *hombre* and Max wondered if that's what he should do later when Rufus was, er, visiting him—pretend he was getting screwed by The King. Yeah, he'd pretend to be Priscilla. Max pledged that if he ever got out of this hole, he'd go straight to Graceland, give his thanks for help in a tight spot. Maybe hang with Priscilla. The babe had mileage but serious bucks—he could use some of that.

He was weeping now, and he knew, dammit, only a real man could allow himself that freedom.

After the slop they called dinner it was lights out. Jesus Christ, Max was sobbing again, begging for his mommy. He wished he'd read more of that fucking Genet book so at least he'd know what to expect. He would've paid a fortune for some Vaseline so at least it wouldn't hurt. But he knew, worse than the pain would be all the fucking humiliation tomorrow, all the guys knowing that Rufus had done the deed. He just hoped that Rufus didn't make him walk around the prison wearing lipstick and fucking skirts, like that queen in *Animal Factory*.

But then something weird happened.

He was waiting for the brute to climb down and deliver the meat, but the bunk was still. Maybe Rufus was just playing head games with him, making him think he wasn't gonna get fucked tonight, then… kaboom.

But another ten, fifteen minutes went by and still no Rufus. And what was that noise? Was he actually *snoring*? The fuck was going on?

Max wanted to feel happy, but he didn't dare let himself. It had to be part of some plan or something. A guard would unlock a bunch of inmates' cells and let them into Max's and the goddamn gangbang would begin.

He waited. At some point, he fell asleep.

In the morning, he woke up and wriggled his ass around a little. No pain. Was it possible he'd slept through being anally raped? It wouldn't have been the first time but, nope, his ass was its good ol' self.

Then another surprise: Rufus hung down from the

top bunk, smiled, asked, "Yo, what up? Sleep good, Mohammed?"

What the fuck? Was this some kinda fuckin' joke? Was this how the guy turned himself on, let his victims think they were off the hook, then, when their guard was fully down…

"Yes," Max said hesitantly.

"That's good," Rufus said. "If there's anythin' you want me to do today, yo, you just let me know, hear, and I get that shit done for you fast, know what I'm sayin'?"

Max had no idea what to make of Rufus's sudden turnaround, but he wasn't complaining. His ass wasn't complaining either.

Then the biggest surprise of all: At breakfast, there was no whistling, no catcalls, no nothing. Shit, people wouldn't even make eye contact with him. The fuck was going on? Yeah, he was glad he hadn't gotten raped, but the insecure Max Fisher was coming out, asking, *Have I, like, lost my appeal?* Other guys in the room were getting the old come-hither looks, guys younger than Max, and he found himself actually feeling jealous.

In the yard, Max went up to one of the guards, Malis, and asked, "The fuck's going on? How come nobody'll fuckin' look at me anymore?"

Malis, chomping on gum, didn't look at Max, said, "The fuck do I know?"

"Come on, give me a fuckin' break," Max whined.

"If this silent treatment is just a set-up, if I'm gonna get ambushed tonight, the least you could do is let me know about it. I'm a well-connected guy, if you get my drift."

Yeah, let the asshole think he was in store for a hefty bribe. Like that was gonna happen.

"You're not gonna get ambushed," Malis said.

"Yeah? How the fuck do you know that?"

Malis continued looking away, chewing his gum, then shook his head as if, thinking, *I give up*, and said, "Look, your story got around, all right?"

"Story? What story?"

"The story about what you got sent away for."

Max was confused, said, "I'm confused."

"All the guys," Malis said, "they know what you did."

"You talking about the drug dealing charges?"

"No, I'm talking about how you cut off that guy's dick down in the city."

The severed dick was a, well, issue that had come up in Max's trial. Max had had nothing to do with it, but apparently the prisoners thought he had. Actually, Angela's latest psycho boyfriend had cut off the dick, delivered it to Max in a shoebox.

"You mean they think I—"

"Everybody's scared shitless," Malis said. "They don't want to come near you. Hey, and just in case you get any ideas, you come anywhere near my dick, I even see you looking at my dick, I'm gonna fuckin' shoot you. Got that?"

It took a while—okay, less than a minute—for it to sink in. He wasn't a target anymore. He was—get this—a feared man.

He took a little spin around the yard, a *victory lap*, soaking it up, letting all the suckers know who the new King was. Wasn't there a movie like that already? *The Fisher King?*

Yeah, he could learn to like this joint.

Five

*"I knew I'd never get enough of her.
She was straight out of hell."*
GIL BREWER, *The Vengeful Virgin*

When Angela and Sebastian got back to the villa, he
was seriously spooked. This was a crazy woman and,
lordy, if he ever got the hell away from her, he might
well write her as a character in his book. The book
he'd never written a line of but he would, he was literary, like Amis and Borroughs. He'd just sit down one
day and *voila*, masterpiece. You either had it or you
didn't and he bloody well had it.

One literary effort that he actually did produce was
a poem in the technical college entitled:

Lenin and Your Letter

He just flat out loved that title. It had politics, love
and, to be totally honest, true resonance. And, okay,
he'd been a little wiped when he wrote it, but excuse
me, look at all the greats—Scott Fitz, Hem, Behan,
Bukowski, Berryman, Jerry Rodriguez. Hadn't they all
been a little, well, spiffed when they wrote their finest
work? You wanted pain, compassion, suffering, Sebastian knew you had to fucking live it.

He just wished he could remember the bloody poem. Only one line had remained with him:

Lenin, you Jewish hack

Ah, the thrill. Did he actually write that? He did. Oh, Booker Prize be praised. And God bless Salman Rushdie. Sebastian had his very brief moment of fame as the student union, all five of them, had accused him of anti-Zionism. Lordy, it was what every real literary lion endured.

Whoops, the deranged bitch was shaking him, not with the cleaver, least not yet, saying, "Hello, shite-face, time to like, you know, clean up?"

And he did, but her language! Was that really necessary? She should go to the U.K. where they mightn't like you but, by golly, they always had manners.

They scrubbed the place down, every last drop of blood, etcetera, gone. Would they bring in forensics of the Greek variety? Hello, let's be honest. The Greek variety of forensics was probably one greasy inspector with his hand out, dropping cigar ash all over the crime scene and trampling on bloodstains. They were clear, and if he could now just get clear of the mad cow he could get his show on the road.

She gave him the golden opportunity, snapped, "Where are my fookin cigs?"

And he jumped on it, said, "Hon, I'll jump on the scooter, get you a fresh pack."

Then, distracted, she said, "And buy some booze, too. Jesus wept."

There was a ferry to Athens—he checked his fake Rolex—in two hours. He put the pedal to the metal and he was out of there. He had a tiny villa rented as close to the port as he could find. He'd learned the hard way, always have your getaway planned. All he needed was his passport, his Cambridge tie, borrowed (so to speak) from a chap—damn tie opened more doors than his wonderful polished BBC accent—his trusty Gladstone bag, one of the few genuine items he owned—and one of those Moleskine diaries, nicely weathered and one of these days, he might actually jot something down in it. He believed he looked suitably battered, had that *climbed the Himalayas and crossed the damn Ganges* look. Made him seem like a Bruce Chatwin traveler type. He hadn't actually read Chatwin, but that hardly mattered. Most of all, he had his stash, the vital element, *the get-out-of-town-and-fucking-fast-old-bean* dosh.

He wouldn't have time to get the deposit back on his little scooter, but as he'd paid with a bum credit card, it was kind of poetic justice; and if he did take the time the psycho bitch would be starting to wonder was he making the bloody cigarettes and come looking.

He shivered, seeing her with that cleaver. God he was sweaty, from fear and stress, the golly goshed heat. He liked to be always, in every sense, cool, but a cleaver can change a lot of habits. He'd had to forego taking a shower in his haste to get out, and he promised himself now that he'd book into the King

Kronos in Athens, get the penthouse, use his Platinum Visa, only ever taken out for real occasions and Jolly Hockey Sticks, this was one of those times.

He threw his Jermyn Street bespoke shirts, his beloved linen suit and Panama hat (his nod to Somerset Maugham—and, truly, he must read the crusty old bugger someday), and splashed some cologne on. Not too much, a hint darlings, not like the mad Paddy he'd met who seemed to climb into the bottle, not only of Jameson but cologne. He sighed, thinking, The Irish. They had not one ounce of restraint.

He went to get his stash, carefully hidden under the loose tile in the shower. *Tipota*, Greek for all gone. Not a bean. The bloody hell was this? And a note. A note?

> *Darling,*
>   *Lest you ever think of running out on me, I'm, shall we say, holding this in trust for you.*
>   *Xxxxxxx*
>   *Love you loads*

Only one time he'd been a little the worse for wear on the old retsina and allowed her to come back to his place and the cunt, she'd cleaned him out.

He checked his wallet. He had his vital credit cards, his return ticket to Athens, and about 200 Euro.

Move, the voice in his head urged.

He did, and fast.

*

Angela, waiting for Sebastian to return with the cigs and booze, was on her hands and knees, scrubbing Georgios' blood, getting a bad case of déjà vu. Yes, somehow it felt like she'd been through this before, but the worst part was this time she'd seen it coming. She was driving along the tunnel, the headlights coming right for her, and the idea that maybe she should, like, *slow down* or, even better, *turn around*, hadn't occurred to her. Falling for a British accent of all things. Couldn't it at least have been an athletic Brit, a David Beckham type? She knew she was posh enough to get any British guy she wanted, but she wound up with fookin' Sebastian. Honestly, she'd never met a bigger wuss, as you'd call it in America. He was so fooking polite, she was just dying to take him to a few bars she knew in Ireland, introduce him to a few guys she knew, they'd make a man out of him all right.

And what about the way he said "lordy" all the time and wore that God-forsaken safari jacket? He looked like an early victim in an Agatha Christie film, the first annoying bastard who gets bumped off. In bed the other night, he'd started reciting some god awful poem, something about a fookin Zionist. Pluck any drunk off the street in Dublin, he could write a better poem than that shite.

Another thing: Would he open his jaw when he talked? Sometimes she'd have sworn his mouth must be wired shut.

Sebastian was useless, no doubt about it, but right now she needed him, to get out of this mess. After they'd dumped the Greek's body off the cliff she'd decided they had to clean up every drop of blood from the villa, then take off *pronto*. One thing Angela knew how to do was run like hell. They both agreed there was no way they could stick around and explain what had happened. The "he raped me and I killed him in self defense" story wouldn't go over well with Greek cops—after all, nearly chopping off a guy's head wasn't exactly like spraying him with mace. She'd taken it a little too far, yeah, so, what else was new?

And where was Sebastian already? She needed ouzo, a whole bottle of it, and how long had he been gone, a half hour already?

The doorbell rang. Finally! What would his excuse be, that he'd soiled his knickers along the way and what a bloody inconvenience it was?

This was the last time she was dating a Brit.

But when she opened the door she saw a woman—dark with almost a full mustache and a unibrow.

"Where is my Georgios?" the woman demanded.

Angela was tempted to say, Atlantis, but went with, "Haven't seen him in a few days." She was very calm, but no surprise there. She was used to this, her experiences in New York and Dublin, lying to the cops, were coming in handy.

The woman's eyes were trying to look past Angela, into the house. Jesus, why had she gone and opened the door without checking first? It was that fecking Sebastian, screwing with her brain.

But one slip-up—shit, she was still holding the rag, the rag with Georgios' blood. She managed to hide it behind her back and didn't think the woman had noticed.

The woman said, "If you're fucking my husband, I kill you."

Husband? It surprised Angela, but only for a second. These Greeks, they always had wives.

Angela checked to make sure the woman wasn't holding a meat cleaver, then said, "I beg your pardon. I mean, I never…"

Sounding seriously miffed.

"Yesterday, he tell me he go here to fix sink," the woman said, "then he don't come home. I know he like you, blondie. Every day he talk about the sexy girl from Ireland."

Squeezing the rag tightly behind her back, Angela said, "First of all, I have a boyfriend, Sebastian, he looks exactly like Lee Child."

The woman was lost.

Angela added, "Secondly, I have no idea where your husband is, but if you want some advice, you should seriously think about divorcing that guy. I've heard stories about him."

She let it hang there.

The woman glared, said, "Stories? What stories?"

Angela exhaled, as if it were killing her to have to

say this, then said, "At the taverna. They're saying your husband's with a new woman every night. He cruises the clubs for American girls or some shite. I was appalled, if you want to know the truth. I don't want to put any ideas in your head, but maybe your husband only *told* you he was coming to fix my sink. Maybe he was really out picking up a girl at a club. You ever think about that?"

The woman was thinking about it now.

Angela continued, "I don't know if you Greeks do divorce, but you should seriously think about ditching that guy. You're a beautiful woman, you can do so much better."

Actually the woman was as fugly as they come, but the compliment seemed to have an effect, at least momentarily. She stood a little straighter, her chin up, said proudly, "Do you really think so?"

"I know so," Angela said, suddenly sounding like a life coach. "Get your hair done, sweetie, buy some new clothes, get a makeover, and start doing things for *you*. You've been doing things for *him* for way too long."

Good thing Angela had watched so much *Oprah* over the years. Finally that shite was coming in handy.

But either the woman wasn't an *Oprah* fan or she suddenly remembered what she'd come here for, because her dark eyes narrowed again and she said, "If you see Georgios, tell him when he comes home his wife is going to kill him."

Tempted to say, Mission accomplished, Angela went with, "I'll do that."

The woman left and the door slammed shut.

Whew, that was close. Angela watched through the window, making sure the woman was gone, then got back to work, scrubbing the floor. Where the hell was Sebastian, that fuck-up? The useless fool been gone at least an hour. The stores were less than five minutes away by moped, was it possible he had gotten lost?

When another hour went by and there was still no sign of him it set in that the stuffy Brit had ditched her. It wasn't exactly unexpected; she knew the wimp wouldn't be able to stand up to the heat, which was why she'd cleaned him out. The spineless bastard! She hoped he drove off a cliff, was feeding the fish like Georgios.

She got the room as clean as it was going to get. She didn't see any blood and even if she'd left some she figured they probably didn't know their DNA from their drachmas on this backward fucking island. She packed her suitcase and hit the road.

Walking to the village, she passed the old woman, and of course got the evil eye. Jeez, the woman was creepy, like some kind of witch. It occurred to Angela that she should have waited until night and left when she couldn't be seen. So, okay, she'd panicked, made one slip-up, what did you expect? She hadn't had a drink in, what, twelve hours? How was a girl supposed to think straight without a little ouzo flowing through her system?

She took a cab to the port on the other, flatter side of the island. She didn't want to have to ride the fecking donkeys down to the docks, but she also wanted to get as far away from the villa and Giorgios' wife as possible. See, her thinking wasn't entirely clouded.

During the ride, the cab driver—he was bald, overweight, with a thick mustache; reminded her of the uncle who'd once molested her—was staring at her in the rearview, literally licking his lips. What was it with these men? At a deserted area where there were lots of dunes and nothing else he pulled over, leaned back, and seemed to be unbuckling his belt.

Angela went Irish, said, "Drive this car right now, or you'll get what yeh deserve, yah fookin' bastard."

The guy had probably never met a woman like Angela before. He recognized that this was the voice of a woman who did not fuck around and with a look of sheer terror he buckled his belt and put the car back in drive.

Then he got a call on his cell, and started looking at Angela in the rearview again. Later, she'd realize that this was another mistake, that she should've gotten out of that car and run like hell.

At the port, Angela found out there was a ferry to Lesbos leaving in a few minutes. She chuckled, thinking, after her recent experiences with men, maybe Lesbos wasn't such a bad idea.

At dusk, the ferry arrived at the Lesbos port and she beelined for the closest taverna, right across from the docks. Finally, ouzo. Jaysus wept, she downed two shots, asked for a third. When the bartender gave her the drink she noticed the two cops. They were standing near the door, looking right at her. She was going to make a run for it, but knew it was pointless. She chugged the last shot, figuring, Might as well go out with a bang.

Six

*"He turned on the TV but he lay on his bed with his
back to it because it was a liar. It held up pictures
and said you could be like them but it didn't
tell you how easily everything fell to pieces."*
MATTHEW STOKOE, Cows

Sino wasn't buying Max Fisher's bullshit, everybody
sayin' he'd cut off a man's dick. Sino knew the only
thing that white *puta* businessman ever cut into was
his goddamn steak at Smith & Wollensky. Lying
maricon.

Yeah, Sino knew lots of *bandajos* like Max Fisher.
He grew up in the South Bronx, by Yankee Stadium.
Shit, this was eighties and early nineties, bro, the glory
days when crack was king and the Bronx wasn't burning,
the shit was already burned. You were growing up in
the Bronx then, you needed some money to get high,
the Stadium was the place to go. Scalping tickets, man,
Sino didn't waste his time with that *mierda*. Serious
pesos was in protection. All those suit-and-tie bitches
would come up to the games in the summer, be in
their Mercedes and BMWs and shit, parking in the
cheap lots, like five blocks away from the stadium.
Now come on, man, what's up with that *loco* shit? Man
has millions of dollars, lives in some damn mansion

somewhere, down on Fifth Avenue, and he can't even pay for stadium parking? *Puta* deserve to get his pesos taken.

Sino and his boy would be hanging out in the lots, going up to the cheap motherfuckers saying, "Want me to watch your car for you during the game? Cost fifty dollars."

Yeah, see what the stingy *bandajo*'s gonna do then. They wanna go to Stadium parking and pay twenty dollars and miss part the game or they wanna pay Sino to not get their car fucked up? Most gringos paid the man, no *problema*, *jefe*, but sometimes a man got cheap, wouldn't pay, or said they were gonna call a cop. Wrong answer, my man. Yeah, if motherfuckers got cheap, they didn't wanna pay, they were gonna pay anyway. Sino and his boy would fuck up the windshield, pop the tires, shit like that. But if they said they was gonna call a cop, shit, that was when the real fun started. Then they got to fuck the guy up, break some bones, see some blood.

This one time, a rich *maricon* from Manhattan, kinda looked like Max Fisher, said he wouldn't pay the money. The *puta* just walked away, laughing, the *maricon* was fuckin' laughing, disrespecting Sino's whole crew and shit. So Sino and his boy took their bats and played some ball, Bronx style. They fucked up that car so bad the junkyard wouldn't even take it.

Later that night, Sino and his was boys were doing some reefer, chilling, corner 153rd and Gerard. Somehow the *maricon* found him out there, was probably going around the neighborhood, looking. He went up to Sino and said, "You're paying to get my car fixed, motherfucker."

Motherfucker. Saying that shit through his nose, sounding like the rich Park Avenue motherfucker he was. And the way he was standing, with his hands on his hips, like he was trying to be bad-ass, calling him out and shit in front of his crew. The stupid *maricon* was in Sino's face, like didn't he know who he was messing with.

Sino's boys, man, they started laughing, tears coming out their eyes. Sino knew they were laughing at the *maricon*, not him, but he didn't like it. Then his boy Paco said, still laughing, "Man, you gonna take that shit?"

Sino wasn't.

First he shot Paco in the head, send a message to the rest of his crew, you laugh at Sino, you gonna get popped. Didn't matter that he and Paco knew each other eighteen years, their *madres* came over from Panama together. Had to set the shit straight with somebody and Sino was sending the message, *I pop my best friend, I can pop all you, so,* chingate, *you better watch your laughin' asses.*

Shooting Paco shut up the rest his crew real quick. Then the *bandajo* that started it all, the white guy, turned, tried to run. Sino put four in the *maricon*'s back. He had one shot left, went up to the guy. He was still on the ground, trying to move, but he couldn't. He was still alive though. He was making noises in his throat and blood was coming out of his mouth. Now *that* shit was funny.

Sino laughed, said to the *maricon*, "Say you sorry, *papi*. Say you sorry and I won't pop you no more."

The *maricon* was trying to talk, making sounds like, "S...sah...sah...sar...sar...sah."

"Can't hear you," Sino said and popped him in the head and walked away.

Yeah, Sino, wished he was on the street right now, had a nine on him. He'd put six in Fisher's back real quick. Listen to him beg and shit first, then put one in his head. Or, nah, would be more fun to kill Fisher with his *manos*, squeeze that little-ass neck till he die. He wouldn't mind fucking Fisher too. *Maricon* got a big flabby ass, just the kind Sino liked. Maybe he'd fuck him first then kill him, or kill him then fuck him. Depends what kinda mood he was in.

Max was settling in all right. Already he had *the rep*, a priceless commodity, and he had fresh-pressed denims every day and it looked like the library gig was as good as his. And they'd be stupid not to give it to him— come on, who knew more about books than The M.A.X.? He'd taken a little spin around the library the other day, told one of the guys working there he was "unimpressed" with the selection. Lots of Grisham and Danielle Steele, but where was the beef? No Eddie

Bunker, no Genet, shit, not even any Tim fucking Willocks. The fuck? They did have the book about the caged bird by that Maya Angelou broad. Max liked the author photo in the back of that one. Maya was a hot-looking older chick all right, but the picture was a head shot, and Max wondered what her body looked like, if she was in shape. He figured an African chick, her hair in braids, wearing some big baggy blousy African thing, she must have a big set in there some-where.

Max was also learning the pecking order, the *food chain* of life in the joint. Like there was a sissy on Tier 2 who washed and ironed Max's demins every damn day, and Max, learning fast, treated him like shit. You're in the game, you gotta play it, right? He had his sleeves rolled up and a pack of Marlboro Red tucked in there, like Jimmy Dean. Yeah, he even had the white T inside his shirt, shining in its whiteness, that sissy sure could starch.

He managed to pick up the yard swagger, the one that strolled slowly, aggression leaking from every pore. Yep, he was living it up, living in the moment like a true Buddhist monk. Just being in the prison, day in and day out, seeing the respect, no, *fear,* in all these fuckers' faces gave him a bigger rush than smoking crack ever had. If anybody even looked at The M.A.X. the wrong way, Max would get into the guy's face, go, "You got a fuckin' problem, motherfucker?" Glaring like Denzel in *Training Day*.

Yeah, no doubt about it, The M.A.X. was The King of fucking Attica. His favorite thing was just to walk around and soak up all the respect and admiration he was getting from everybody. Sometimes Max would have some extra fun with it, suddenly rushing up to some fuck's crotch and making a snip-snip motion with his fingers. Man, the assholes looked like they were gonna shit their pants and Max would start laughing his ass off.

In the yard, when The M.A.X. came by people stopped whatever they were doing and they'd say, "Yo, Max," and "What up, Max, man?" It seemed like the whole prison was in awe of him. Well, except for one little hitch.

The population had to be eighty percent black, but there were pockets of other ethnic groups. There were the Crips, Sino's crew of, what're you supposed to call them this week, Latinos, Hispanics, Latin Americans? What the fuck ever. There were also some white people, mostly sissies, but also The Aryan Brotherhood, led by a massive cracker with a whole crew of mutants straight out of *The Hills Have Eyes*, their mouths drooling and always giggling and cussing among themselves.

Jeez, was that English?

He knew these guys didn't give a shit if he once cut off a man's dick or not. These freaks probably chopped off dicks on a regular basis.

The cracker's name was Arma—short for Arma-

geddon. What was up with these deranged assholes
shortening their names? Max wondered if she should
shorten his name, start calling himself "The Ma." Maybe
that would get him even more respect. Nah, it would
probably have the opposite effect. Didn't Freud say all
guys wanted to fuck their mothers?

If anything he should start calling himself The Ax.
Had a menacing vibe to it.

Nah, had to be The M.A.X.

Arma fronted Max in the yard, his Aryan brothers
all around him, went, "You-all's the dick cutter, right?"

Max didn't feel the time was right to say, *Gram-
matically speaking, there is only one of me.* The guy
didn't exactly look like he had a sense of humor.

He nodded, his throat choked from fear. This guy
had the dead-eyed stare of a fucking serial killer.

The guy said, "Y'all shacked up with the big dumb
nigger, what's with that boy?"

And Max, to his amazement, lied. "I'm working on
the inside, we gonna bring them apes into line, we
gotta know what they're planning, you cool with that?"

The guy stared at him and it was up for grabs. He'd
either gut Max right there or…

He laughed, exposing a whole row of yellowed teeth
and many, many gaps. All that moonshine, no doubt.
All around him, the brothers laughed along.

Arma slapped Max on the shoulder, said, "You-all's
one bright fellah. You was one of them high flyers,
m'I right?'

Max, so relieved he nearly wet himself, said, "I made my moola off the niggers. We gonna go up against Zog, we need serious bucks."

Zog? He had no idea really what this meant but on the Discovery Channel he'd heard a Klansman say it.

But, shit, it fuckin' worked.

And then Max on a roll, tried, "The crips, they're gonna move against you, soon."

The riot that was to come down the pike got its seeds right there with Max spouting off crap he'd no idea about.

The cracker frowned, asked, "Them Mex gangs, Sino and 'em, they got weapons?"

Max nodded, as if he couldn't take the risk on verbalizing the lethal threat.

The cracker handed him a leather band, said, "You wear that, you're part of my crew, ain't no one gonna fuck with you."

Max, learning, improvising all the time, took the pack of Reds, handed them over, said, "On me, bro."

Smokes were the currency of the yard. A pack could get you a sissy for a night, a carton would get you anyone wasted.

Arma and his Nazis moved off, the cracker saying, Them Crips come gunning, you're gonna be my right hand guy.

Max thought, Like fuck, but just wanted to get away.

He said, "You can count on me, bro."

o

Later, at lunch, Sino sat down next to Max, smiled, went, "Man, I gotta give you props, yo. Cuttin' off a man's dick? That shit's cold. Even Sino never done shit like that."

Max glared at him, the look he'd been practicing, the one that said, *I'm a cold detached psycho motherfucker, a fuckin Aryan, and y'all better not fuck with me*. Then he gave him a sudden smile, throwing him a bone, and said, "Yeah, what can I tell you? I was havin' a bad day."

Sino smiled, said, "Yeah, tell me all about it, cuz. Like how'd you do it? You use a blade, scissors, hedge clipper, what?"

Max, unprepared for the questioning, said, "Saw."

"Saw? Fuck, man, how'd you work that shit out? You say to the *puta*, put your dick out on the table, I wanna saw it off, and the *bandajo* go, 'Yeah, all right, cut my dick off,' and took down his *pantalones*?"

"Yeah," Max said. "Something like that."

"Oh, it was somethin' like that, huh?" He was still smiling. "So now you don't know for sure? Yeah, guess that makes sense. Scary motherfucker like you, goin' 'round, cuttin' dicks off with saws all the time, you might start to forget some shit, right?"

Max was thinking, *Don't give in. He's just toying with you. Truth is he's scared shitless and he's trying not to show it*.

Glaring hard, Max said, "I cut off his dick with a saw because I didn't like the way he was looking at me, and

I don't like the way you're looking at me right now, *hombre.*"

That was the way—throw the Spanish shit right back at him. Man, he felt like John Wayne, Eastwood, The Rock—somebody bad-ass.

Sino laughed, still trying not to show his weakness, said, "Yeah, you're a scary motherfucker all right, Fisher. Just sittin' here next to you, I'm starting to piss up my pants and shit." Then he touched the leather band on Max's wrist and said, "I see you make some friends today. So now you're what, a motherfuckin' Nazi?"

If cigarettes were the currency of prison, then desserts were the icing on the cake. Max had heard about guys being shanked for a rice pudding. You wanted a favor, you slid your dessert across the table to the guy you wanted the favor from. Today's delicacy was some kind of treacle pie, and Sino's and Max's were lined up in front of them. It was a sign of real juice to just let it sit there, as if just any old con could stroll up and grab it. Yeah, dream on.

Like two fortresses waiting to be attacked, a type of lethal jailhouse chess, Max and Sino stared at each other. Who'd move first? Sino, who didn't exactly seem like the patient type, made a move for one and Max, said, "You don't want to do that, *hombre.*"

He was as amazed as Sino was. Did he just, like, call Sino out?

Sino, his spoon almost ready to dip, hesitated. Bad move. You start a move in the joint, you have to make the play, no turning back. Sino cursed, then went, "Don't call me *hombre*. You ain't my *hombre*. *Entiendes?*"

Max, exhilarated at his sheer *cojones*, said, "I'm thinking I might bring that pie to my main guy, Rufus."

And with that, he stood up, took both pies, *winked* at Sino, said, "Y'all keep it in your pants now, hear, pilgrim."

Sino was too stunned to move. Meanwhile, Max went on his way, clueless that he'd just fanned the flames of an inferno that would rage with biblical ferocity.

Max placed the pies on Rufus's bunk and the huge black man, who'd never seen two desserts in one place, was seriously impressed, asked, "How the fuck you get two?"

Max, adopting his lotus position, grabbing some of that inner peace, said, "Took 'em off that little punk, Sino."

Rufus, adopting the lotus position now, though his bulk made it somewhat difficult, wonderingly asked, "We talkin' the same Sino? Leader of the Crips?"

Max, closing his eyes, said, in total indifference, "That who he is? I bitch slapped him for giving me mouth."

Max had already scared Rufus shitless with the dick-cutting rumor, but now Rufus stared at Max like he was looking at a mini-Manson, obvious admiration leaking from every inch of his massive frame.

Yeah, he was a believer.

Seven

"Lord Byron once said of Polidori that he was the sort of man to whom, if he fell overboard, one would offer a straw, to see if the adage was true that drowning men clutch at straws."
PERCY BYSSHE SHELLEY, IN A LETTER TO HIS
PUBLISHER, JOHN MURRAY (1819)

Sebastian was at Athens airport. He'd been in a bit of a panic until he arrived in Athens, all his rat instincts shouting, Get to the bloody airport.

Finally did and, oh lordy, British Airways, God bless them, took his dodgy Platinum card without a murmur.

The woman at the counter asked, "Business class?"

He gave his best old-school smile, asked, "Is there any other way to fly?"

They had a good Brit chuckle about this.

He was whistling *Rule, Britannia* as he headed for the First Class Lounge, throwing a look of contempt to the, well, sorry, but let's call them what they were, peasants, as they scuttled along for their economy seats.

He sat in the plush armchair, thought, *C'est la vie*.

This was the extent of his French and he tended to ration it. Though, come to think of it, perhaps Paris might be worth a gander. They still loved the Brits, though it was a shame the buggers had banned British beef, as if there was a better meat in the whole world.

He ordered a Campari and soda, didn't say please. A true gent never said please to the help. He was just about to have a large sip when a very attractive blond girl in her twenties approached, asked, "I'm so sorry to bother you, Mr. Child?"

Child? The bloody hell was this? Then he spotted the paperback book in her hand. A thriller of some sort, written by that Lee Child fellow whom Sebastian had been mistaken for on several occasions. He was about to tell the woman to bugger off when she held out the book and said, "I'd be so honored to have your autograph, Mr. Child.

He gave her his most radiant smile, said, "Call me Lee. And the honor is mine, I assure you."

She handed over the book and a pen. It was a Mont Blanc and he thought, *Money*. Then he thought, *Mile-High Club*.

Seeing as how the blushing woman was obviously convinced he was this writer fellow and just as obviously idolized him, he didn't think a little joint trip to the loo would be hard to pull off at all. He scribbled an illegible scrawl on the book's title page like a real pro, and added a little heart. Touch of class. You couldn't teach that, either it came naturally or it didn't come at all.

He handed her back the book, holding the pen as if he'd forgotten it, asked, "Dare I be so bold as to offer you a refreshment?"

She blushed an even deeper shade of crimson and he thought, *Gotcha*.

She was so flustered, flattered, she never even saw

him slip the pen into his jacket. He had one tricky moment after she'd had her second vodka tonic when she asked, "What's next for Reacher?" But he rallied, gave the enigmatic smile that had lured more quail than he could count into the sack, and said, "Now my dear, that would be telling."

They had champagne cocktails after takeoff and he looked out at the cloud of pollution over Athens and thought about the American psycho bitch back on the island. She was probably still wondering where her cigs were.

He had to stifle a laugh, turned to the girl, asked, "What say you, my sweet, to another champers before dinner?"

Her glassy eyes as she nodded yes told him he was about to join the Club.

Later, after he'd rogered her, they crept back to their seats and he got a knowing look from the stewardess. Or was she giving him the *come on*? Sorry, gell, but he was shagged out. A chap had only so much to go round.

The girl snuggled up in her seat and was out in minutes. He waited till they dimmed the lights then went through her handbag. Ah, let's have a look, shall we? Lots of crisp 50 sterling notes and a batch of credit cards. He took only two, a chap wasn't greedy. He ordered a brandy, and some snacks, sat back to watch the movie, something starring Will Ferrell. This chap was in every movie, it seemed.

He started to nod off and had the familiar dream,

the one about the student he'd killed. Sweat was rolling
down his face as he relived the awful events.

Richard had been one of those upper-class pillow
biters, the real deal, descended from one of the families
related to the Royals. Well, who wasn't? But he was
about 1,000 in line to the throne, meaning only 999
buggers had to croak before Richard got a shot at it.

And, lordy, the chap was loaded, had buckets of
dosh. And generous with it, too, spent it like it was
water. Sebastian hated him, damn scoundrel had it all.
But Richard fell in love with Sebastian, who encour-
aged him in the belief that buggery was definitely in
the cards. Meanwhile, pay the freight you bloody homo.

Richard, like all blue bloods, had access to the best
drugs, clubs, people; all of which was damn hunky
fucking dory with Sebby. Yeah, what Richard called
him. He'd pick out a suit from his closet, a beautiful
Jermyn Street made-to-measure beauty and say, "I'm
tired of this, Sebby, you have it," and throw it across
the room to him.

Time came to pay the freight, Sebastian was almost
ready to let it happen. It was a Brit tradition, how else
could you explain the whole Public School system?

They'd been partying hard, lots of the old champers,
a little nose candy to chill out. They ended up back in
Richard's lovely flat.

First false note, Richard had ordered, not asked,
"Pour me a Gordon's."

It was the imperious tone that irritated Sebastian to
no end.

Sebastian, a little the worse for wear, snapped, "What am I? Your servant?"

And Richard, in that totally dismissive accent, said, "You're the help, darling, a leech. So once you get the drinkie-poos, hop over here, Sebby, and service my Lancelot."

He had a name for his dick? Well, all right, who didn't. But he also had a name for Sebastian, and it was the more demeaning of the two.

Sebastian lost it, strangled the upper class twit with his Eton tie, screaming,

"Don't you dare call me Sebby!"

And then horrified, strung him up from the light fixture, took all the available cash and yes, a few suits and ties, and prayed to everything unholy that he'd get away, that he'd, dare one say, *swing it.*

The family hushed it all up. Sebastian even read the eulogy at the very private mass, quoted a passage from Wilfred Owen.

Later, when he saw the movie *The Talented Mr. Ripley*, he so identified with Matt Damon, he almost shouted: *I'm with you, old chap!*

Eight

*"Cuccia was angry that he would have to renegotiate
the price of a hit gone wrong, he would be dealing
from a very weak hand."*
CHARLIE STELLA, *Charlie Opera*

After that shit in the mess hall, with the *bandajo* Max
Fisher takin' all his pies, and his whole crew sittin'
there, watching like, You gonna take that shit? Sino
knew he had to make a move. Shit, not only was he
dissed, but he got *called* by that white pudgy middle-
aged white motherfucker.

His face burned, man, rage. He swore on his *abuela*'s
life, he'd gut this white trash from his balding head to
his tiny dick. He knew he'd have to act and fast, to be
crewless was to be chowder. Yeah, he'd love to do
Fisher himself, but that wasn't the way it was done.
When you were the main man in charge of a whole
crew, you told people to do shit, you never did it yourself. White people had a name for that shit. Out
saucering? Yeah, he was gonna out saucer this shit.

In the yard, he spotted a new fish, kid named
Carlito. *Puta*'s first day, looked like somebody'd
already cut him a new asshole. The *bandajo*'d been

caught driving a stolen car, first time. Man was Mex
and got the max, five and change.

Yeah, was time to make the man earn his way in.

Carlito stood with his back to the wall. He'd been told
about the train and couldn't get Tom Hanks in that
goddamn movie, going *All aboard the train*, out of his
mind. He'd been told his only hope was to join a gang
in, like, Speedy Gonzales time. But how the fuck did
you join? He'd seen the Crips, and the other gangs, all
giving him the dead eye, not like he could wander up,
go, "What's shakin', dudes? And, oh, I wanna join the
gang."

Then he saw a dangerous-looking one heading his
way. The guy was smiling, like a Great White, put out
his hand, said, "*Muchacho*, how's it hanging, boss?"

As Carlito took it and felt the man squeeze real
tight, Carlito tried to figure out where it had all gone
down the shitter. He'd had a nice lady, girl named
Maria, and she'd been making marriage sounds. She
was such a sweet *senorita*, they grew up together in
Guadalajara. He was making seven bucks an hour
from his job in the garage. Yeah, the garage—he knew
cars, and that was how the shit hit the fan.

Maria had gone to see her Mama and Carlito had
decided to let off a little steam. He'd been pulling
twelve-hour shifts, getting the down payment ready on
a little apartment, and Dios Mio, he was wound up
awful tight, so he got together with a few *amigos*, they
were downing some Dos Equis, nice and cold and

going down so easy, till one of the *hombres* ordered up shots of Tequila. Carlito was basically a beer and chips kinda guy, but he didn't want to look bad, like some *maricon*, so he had the shot and then, Madre Mio, a whole lot more and he didn't know, they were falling out of the bar, laughing and high fiving, when one of the *hombres* spotted the Firebird, red and with the keys in the ignition. The owner gone to the ATM. Next thing, Carlito was driving the baby, like he owned the highway. State Trooper chased him for half an hour before the bird ran outa gas and Carlito ran shit out of luck.

He'd paid all of their savings to a slimy lawyer who promised, "Probation, no problem, first offense, *no problema.*"

He got five years and change. *No problema?*

The lawyer shrugged, said, "You got any more of that there green, I'll lodge an appeal."

Maria had taken off with the few remaining dollars and Carlito got to ride the bus.

Scared, chained, out of it. A guy sitting beside him asked, "First time, *chiquito?*"

He nodded in total misery.

The guy, covered in prison tats, said, "You're a real pretty boy, they gonna ream you good, *compadre.*"

The guy was staring at Carlito's solid gold Miraculous Medal. Carlito, with difficulty, using his manacled hands, tried to button the prison-issue shirt and the guy laughed, a laugh born of pure nastiness and worse, deep malevolent knowing, said, "First day in the joint, it's like, every worst nightmare you ever had and bro, it's worse, 'cause it's true and it ain't gonna git no better, so you do what you can, you get wasted, you hear me, fish, you gotta get some serious dope going in your system—then it don't, like, hurt. Me, I got my main running buddy up there, he'll hook me up right after orientation, and you wanna, you want some of that good stuff, help you *get focused*, you come see me, I fix you right up but it costs, you know what I'm sayin'?"

He shut up for a bit then said, "Speed. The ol' reliable, amphetamines, they set you right up and Bennies, ain't nuttin on God's good earth like those beauties."

He laughed, obviously feeling the effect of some of the above, began to sing, "Benny and the Jets." Was it horrible, man, or what? Even worse than having to hear Elt himself do it.

The guy added, "That there medal, always wanted me one of those babes. You want some *recreational drugs?* That there is the freight, *muchacho*."

Carlito snapped himself out of his reverie, tried to pay attention to the guy holding onto his hand. Leader of the Crips. His mouth went dry and he smiled like some wetback fresh from the border.

Sino swept his arm round the yard, said, "Who you with?" Then in a mocking tone, continued. "I tell you, fish, you with nobody. You got, like, *de nada*, you hear me, fish?'

Carlito did.

Sino said, "See those *hombres* over there? Yeah, the ones lookin' at you, like you a big juicy *empanada*. They gonna run a line through yo skinny ass, you don't be with somebody."

Carlito was already crying, bawling like a damn baby.

Sino moved in close, said, "Yo, you join my crew, you be safe, know what I'm talkin' about?"

Carlito nodded. He'd have joined the army at this stage. Anything. Sino palmed him a toothbrush, hand-made blade embedded on the top, said, "Yo, you wanna make some bones, you show yo' got *cojones*. Know what I talkin' about, *jefe*?"

Carlito wanted to run, but where?

Sino looked at his watch, a shiny TAG Heuer knock-off, said, "Twelve noon, fat middle-aged white dude, takes his shower on C…you go rip him a new one, *comprende*?"

Sino sauntered off and Carlito began a whole new set of tremors.

At twelve noon Carlito headed to the showers. He'd managed to score some bennies from the guy he'd rode the bus up with. Cost him his gold Miraculous Medal he'd always worn. In a haze of drug-induced adrenaline and outright fear, he saw the fat white dude and launched himself. The phrase *It got away from him* might be appropriate here. He was still slashing and chopping when the guards clubbed him senseless. One of them, who'd seen most all a prison could offer, muttered, "Holy Mother of Christ."

And too bad for Sino, what remained of the fat dude on the shower floor was the armaments guy for the Aryan Brotherhood.

Carlito heard another guard say, "*Hombre*, you just fucked yourself good," and everything faded out.

Nine

"A caged woman is a beast of ferocious instinct."
SEÑOR RODRIGUEZ

When they brought Angela to the prison in Lesbos her first thought was, Jaysus, this place lives up to its name. She was brought to a holding cell with eight other women. Each was hotter than the last and most of them were in micro-minis, skimpy tube tops, a couple even in bikinis. Most were talking in Greek, and a couple of blondes were talking in some other language, maybe Swedish.

Angela went up to one of the blondes and asked for a smoke. Jaysus, with the day she'd had, she could've used a whole carton.

The woman's friend, the other Swede, slid one out of a pack.

Angela took it, held it out for a light, said, "I'm Angela."

"Inga," the woman with the cigarettes said. "This is Katina."

Angela asked, "So is this a prison or a nightclub?"

Thought she was making a joke, but Katina said, "Both."

"There was a raid at Niko's last night," Inga explained. "Heroin or something."

"But we have nothing to do with it," Katina said.

She sounded a little too defensive. Angela glanced down, noticed the track marks on her skinny arms.

"Yes, we were just there, you know, partying, when the police come," Inga said. "How do you say, the wrong places at the wrong times?"

Thinking, *The story of me life*, Angela asked, "So what did they charge you with?"

"We do not know what's going on," Inga said. "They told us nothing. They just bring us here, that's it."

"We are, how do you say," Katina said, "in the dark."

"What about you?" Inga asked. "What did you do?"

"Oh, nothing," Angela said. "I was just having a drink, minding my own business, and next thing I knew two cops were taking me away."

"It's crazy in Greece," Katina said. "They arrest everybody, no?"

The prison wasn't like any prison Angela had ever heard of. The officers who'd arrested Angela hadn't notified her of any charges, or at least she didn't think they had. During the ride over they were talking in Greek and the only parts Angela picked up were when they were commenting on her *oreo megala vizia*—big, beautiful tits—no surprise there. But, of course, Angela knew why she was being taken away. The cab driver on Santorini must've told the authorities that she'd boarded a boat for Lesbos and then the Lesbos police—Lesbian police? Jaysus, it sounded like something out of Greenwich Village, but that was probably what they called themselves—had been notified. They were probably just waiting now to coordinate with the Santorini cops. She didn't know if they'd found some evidence that could hang her or if she was just a suspect by default. Not that it mattered. She'd heard enough stories over the years from her father about the Greek justice system. It was your classic, old-world, eye-for-an-eye, guilty-until-proven-innocent mentality. She figured she'd never be formally charged with anything. She'd be handed over to Georgios' relatives and quietly killed, case closed.

Fookin' Sebastian. If he hadn't run off like the coward he was, she never would've had to take that cab to the other end of Santorini. They would've ridden together on the moped and she wouldn't be in this shithole right now. They hadn't even let her make a phone call. Not that there was anyone to call. A lawyer would be useless and her family was even more so. Her mother's side was all ex-IRA and her father's side was as backward as Georgios' family.

"Do any of the guards here speak English?" Angela asked.

"There was a young guy here last night," Inga said, "maybe nineteen years old. He was hitting on all the women."

"He told one girl, if she give him blowjob she can get out," Katina said as she casually reached out and held Inga's hand. "He is like a teenage boy, his eyes jumping out of his head with so many beautiful women.

He even offered to pay, fifty euro, keeps showing it, pulls money out of this belt tied round his waist. Keeps zipping and unzipping the belt, saying 'Want what's in here?' Pig."

Angela thought, *Bingo*.

Angela asked Katina, "When does his shift start?"

The girl shrugged, said, "Night."

Angela looked around the cell, which was getting hotter and less comfortable as the sun rose. She said, "How do you pass the time in here?" and then got strange looks from the girls and thought, Uh-oh.

Sure enough, by the time the scorching midday heat hit top level, the sun blasting through the bars, the other women, who hadn't been wearing all that much to begin with, began unbuttoning their shirts, rolling up their sleeves, pulling off sweat-stained clothes. Angela watched one woman roll her tube top down to her waist and lie down on one of the cell's two metal bunks. It was like a signal to the others—in minutes, all eight women had stripped down. The two girls who'd been in bikinis tossed their tops in a corner of the cell and sat down side by side in a patch of sunlight, one with her arm around the other's waist. A very large Russian woman took off her blouse, revealing a skimpy bra through which Angela could make out a tattoo in the shape of an eagle across the woman's breasts. Jaysus, this fookin' Lesbos more than lived up to its name. Too bad Angela was straight or she wouldn't've been in such a hurry to get out of this place.

Inga lit another cigarette, inhaled deeply, then passed it to Katina. The Russian woman came over, started stroking Katina's arm, kissing her neck. She looked at Angela, and purred, "You like?"

Angela shrugged, moved to the water bucket, thinking, Whatever turns you on, lady. As Angela used a dirty towel to wipe off her face, she could see the women pairing off on the floor, the bunks, standing against the wall.

She found an empty corner and sat down, closed her eyes, but it didn't stop her hearing the sounds around her. She bit down on her lower lip and focused on two things: the young guard and, especially, the money belt.

At midnight, the kid arrived and, Jaysus, the Swedes were right, he seemed like a child let loose in a candy shop. He had an overall deranged look about him, as if someone had hit him in the head with a baseball bat and he was wandering around, permanently dazed. But when it came to men sometimes Angela wasn't exactly picky. Hell, she'd been engaged to Max Fisher, hadn't she?

The important thing was that the kid was the only guard on duty at night and sure enough, he was wearing the money belt.

Angela knew she had to work fast. She was surprised no one from Georgios' family had shown up yet, but it was only a matter of time. She figured she had till morning, tops.

When the kid came by all the women spoke at once,

complaining, demanding to be released. But Angela caught his attention, pursing her lips and batting her eyelashes, doing her best Marilyn Monroe come-hither look. Okay, so maybe she was overdoing it, but it worked, didn't it?

The kid came right over and Angela whispered, "So what does a girl have to do to get out of this place?"

The kid smiled. Jaysus, panted, "Come with me." He opened and closed the cell door with a giant skeleton key.

They went into what you'd call the office. There was a desk, a chair, and not much else. The walls were corroded and a fan was spinning haltingly overhead.

"Get naked," the kid said.

Usually it was a turn-on for Angela when the guy ordered her around, but not this time.

"I thought you'd want a little…" she looked at his crotch "…lip service."

"You kill somebody," the kid said. "If you steal, blowjob, okay, but you kill, you have to fuck."

Angela had a feeling arguing this logic would be pointless. Besides, it wasn't like she had a lot of bargaining power.

They went at it—or rather he went at it—for what seemed like three or four hours. He wasn't the worst she'd ever had, but that was only thanks to Max Fisher. The kid was lost, in his own world; she could've died and he wouldn't have noticed. At one point she had a flashback to Georgios and she had the temptation to reach up, grab the kid's head, and snap his neck.

Thank God she resisted. She was in enough trouble, and killing a fookin' prison guard wouldn't exactly improve her situation.

Finally it ended, and the kid, like every goddamn man Anglela had ever known, fell asleep. She took his money belt, got his keys and then on impulse, picked up one of his heavy boots from where he'd tossed it before climbing on top of her, walloped him upside the head with it, said, "We call that cold cocked."

She had to move fast. Did she think of releasing the other women? Did she fuck. It was every bitch for their own selves.

She was exhausted, and as she headed toward the docks she thought about how she'd gotten here, to this low point in her life. A few years ago, things had been going so well for her. It seemed like just yesterday she was living in New York, working as an executive assistant, dating guys, living in a studio apartment in Gramercy Park. Yeah, she'd made a few bad decisions—a few spectacularly bad decisions—but did she really deserve *this*?

She boarded a ferry to Naples. As the boat pulled away, she yelled, "Greece, you can kiss my Irish arse goodbye!"

She remained in the back of the ferry staring half-dazed, watching until the lighthouse at the tip of Lesbos faded to nothing. Good fookin' riddance.

She counted the money from the kid's belt, was surprised to find nearly two thousand euro. It'd be enough for a new outfit and a plane ticket, so sayonara you bastards, she was getting the first flight out of this shithole and back to the States.

Of course then she'd be nearly broke again. But she knew that Max, the little bollix, he'd have money stashed and if she was in that place of total desperation she could do whatever it took to get hold of it. Then, just maybe she could use the stake she got to set up something to sustain her till she could come up with a longer-term plan.

Right there and then, she'd have killed for some lip gloss and perfume. She could still smell the guard. She was tempted to jump into the sea and wash herself clean.

Say what you want about Greek ferries, they have one great feature—a bar.

She headed down there, ignored various suggestions from the motley crew and ordered a large Metaxa. The barman leered at her and she gave him a look that no doubt withered his coming hard-on.

He muttered, *"Mallakismeni."*

Yeah, like she gave a shit.

Over in a corner, she saw a girl in her very early twenties, sobbing quietly. She looked pale—maybe English, maybe a fucking albino—and broken.

Angela thought, *Welcome to my world, honey.* Had one motherfooker, like, ever helped her out? Was there one cocksucker on the whole planet who hadn't fooked her over in some way? Nope, not one lousy decent human on the planet. She thought, You paddle your own frigging canoe, no time like the present to learn that life sucks and if you were a single woman, guess who gets to do the sucking?

Still, there was a good heart in Angela once upon a time and it still flickered—dimly, but there.

She approached, asked, "Join you, girl?"

The girl looked up, looking relieved to see not only a woman, but an American. She began to weep profusely, said, "Oh, please do."

The British accent reminded her of Sebastian, but Angela was still sympathetic. She drank off half her brandy and Christ, it burned, bitter and with a kick like a Santorini mule. Which was why she was drinking the shite.

She offered the remainder to the girl, who protested, "Isn't it a little early?"

Such a Brit.

Angela said, "Darlin', it's been too late for you and me since we landed in this fooking country."

For a moment the girl seemed startled at the profanity and then they both began to laugh, prompting the Greek men at the bar to throw the evil eye at them. Nothing scarier for a macho type than the sound of women's laughter. They fear it's directed at them and they're mostly right.

The girl told Angela the usual tired story, boyfriend fooked off with their cash. Same sad song, same sad result, and all she had was her return ticket on the ferry

Angela would never quite know why she asked, "How much is the airfare home?"

Stunned, the girl said she could get a cheap flight for maybe three hundred euro.

Angela gave her four hundred, gripped her hand tightly and said, "Buy yourself a nice dress, have a meal and get home as if the devil was chasing you."

Ten

*"Riots generally had no causes, or the causes were pretty small,
like a particularly bad meal in the mess hall."*
PATRICIA HIGHSMITH, *The Glass Cell*

Violence was in the air in Attica, you could practically
smell it. After the Aryan was found dead in the shower,
rumor spread that Sino's crew was behind it. Two days
later Carlito, the Mexican kid, was found dead in the
shower—his throat slashed after he'd been gang raped.
Max felt sorry for him, but, come on, what did the
moron expect, going up against the Brotherhood with
nothing but a sharpened toothbrush? Hadn't he boned
up on prison literature before he got sent away? Eh,
not everybody could be as savvy and as street smart
as The M.A.X.

Rumors were spreading that when Sino got out of
the hole the Aryans were gonna make their big move.
Rufus and his boys were planning to get in on the fun,
and the spic gangs and the Bloods were going to get
their licks in, too. Max could hardly contain himself—
a major prison uprising was brewing! Riots at Attica, it
was so fuckin' Pacino. Someday, when they filmed the
story of his life, the riots would be the fucking set

piece. It was going to be biblical, historical, and Max Fisher was going to be in the middle of it all.

One morning, when Sino had been away in the hole for about a week, the mail guy came by Max's cell, held out an envelope, and said, "Fisher."

Max was surprised to hear his name called. Rufus got letters all the time from God knows who, but so far Max had gotten *nada*. After all, who was there to write him? He didn't expect to hear from his relatives, that was for sure. They all said he'd disgraced the family, they never wanted anything to do with him again, yadda yadda yadda. As far as Max was concerned, that was fine with him. His brother called him a loser and a lowlife. Jesus Christ, the guy was a fucking teacher and he was calling *Max* a loser? Come on.

Max was a big-time criminal, a fucking celebrity. He figured there had to be, like, dozens of websites devoted to him, and blogs, and, hell, fan clubs. Maybe the letter was from one of his fan club members.

Max looked at the return address: Paula Segal.

His first thought: *Somebody I banged?*

Yeah, probably. He'd had so many conquests over the years, how could he keep track? Now that he was famous, now that he'd made it, she probably wanted to weasel in, score some of his dough for herself. Yeah, like that was gonna happen. His ex-wife had taught him all about pre-nups.

He opened the envelope—there was a note and, oh yeah, baby, a picture. And, whoa, hold the phones, this chick was hot! After nearly three weeks in lockup, Rufus was looking better to him every night—but this girl, fuck, she was a serious knockout. Okay, Max hadn't looked at her face yet, but those huge gazongas, had to be 36-C's at least, maybe D's. They were high, too, and he liked the way they were squished together in that little swimsuit, and so tight you could bounce a quarter off 'em.

Finally, after maybe a minute or two, he looked at her face. Nah, she didn't look like an ex, but that didn't mean anything. Would Hef recognize all of his conquests? When you were a big-time player like Max Fisher, women tended to blur.

He skimmed the note, something how she was a writer, knew some other chicks—Laura Lippman, Tess Gerritsen, hopefully they were stacked too—and, holy shit, she wanted to write his life story. See, Hollywood was calling, and sooner than he'd expected. Yeah, it was all coming together, just at its own pace, that's all. He was already the most feared man at Attica, and now some hot babe from Manhattan, a big-time writer, was all over him. Obviously she'd want to fuck him. She had to get to know her subject as well as she could, didn't she?

As soon as he could get his hands on some paper and a pen, Max wrote:

Dear Paula,
    Love the picture!!!!
    As you can imagine I get A LOT of requests like

*this. James Patterson wanted to write my story, but
I said, No, thanks, Jimmy, way too busy.*

*That said, drop by and I'll squeeze you in. Just
make sure you wear something like in the picture.*

Love,

The M.A.X.

P.S. Bring Laura and Tess. The more the merrier.

A few days later, Max was called down to the visitor's
room. He had his hair slicked and a rolled-up sock in
his crotch—yeah he was ready to rock 'n' roll.

There was only one chick there, Paula, but, man,
she looked even hotter in person. For the last couple
of nights, Max had been jerking off, imagining this
moment, and talk about living up to a fantasy. She was
in a low-cut top, loose enough that you could almost
see her nipples. Man, if the glass wasn't there he
wouldn't've been able to resist. He would've just
reached out and grabbed 'em.

He stared at her tits for a while longer, then realized
she was talking to him. He put on a headset, heard:

"Mr. Fisher, I can't tell you what a pleasure it is to
meet you. I've read everything about you I could get
my hands on. I was at your trial, but I didn't have the
opportunity to introduce myself. Thank you so much
for agreeing to meet me here, and fit me into your tight
schedule. I can't tell you how much I appreciate it."

Jesus, Max thought, she was like a bad date—she
never shuts up.

But he smiled, had to keep up his celebrity persona,

and said, "You have great tits, but you've probably heard that dozens of times before, right?"

She smiled. What, she thought he was joking? Then she said, "I've booked a motel room in the area. I was hoping we could talk once a day over the course of the next several weeks. I'm trying to arrange with the warden a better place to meet, face-to-face, in private. He said it requires some arrangement, but hopefully it's something that could happen soon. I'm just so…"

Max was looking at her rack again. Fuck, they were so close yet so far away.

"You single?" he asked.

She hesitated, then said, "Yes. Yes, I am."

"Me, too," Max said. "See? We already have something in common." He laughed then added, "I want to proposition you." He realized that didn't come out right and said, "I mean, I want to make a proposition *to* you. Me and you, we seem to get along, right? We have a lot in common, make each other laugh. I was thinking, how about we, you know, get married?"

Why was she laughing? Eh, she was probably just so happy she couldn't contain herself. That had to be it.

"Hey, don't get too excited," he said. "There'll be a pre-nup—a *serious* pre-nup. If you think I'm gonna give you half the Fisher fortune, think again, *muchacha*. I made that mistake once and I'm sure as shit not gonna make it again. But, yeah, it'll be great to be married to you because me and you, we could have those, what do they call them, congenital visits? No, that's not it. Conjugal visits. Yeah, we'll have those."

Max had been thinking about his herpes, but she didn't have to know about that. Things were going so well, there was no reason to ruin the mood.

"I don't know what to say," Paula said.

God, were her tits, like, growing?

"Say yes," Max said.

"I'm very flattered, obviously," she said. "I mean, you're a very attractive man, and I'm so honored that you're taking the time to—"

"Look, honey, you want me to write this book with you, don't you?"

He liked that—let the not-so-subtle threat hang there. That was the way to play hardball with the literary bitch. After all, not only had he cut off a man's dick—yeah, he was starting to believe it himself—he was the king of Attica, a feared man, and he might as well start fucking acting like it, right? You want The M.A.X. to give something, you gotta give him something in return.

Like that.

"I'll think it over," she said. "In the meantime, I was hoping we could—"

"I look like Chris Rock?" Max asked.

Paula looked confused, said, "I'm confused."

"I look like Chris Rock?" Max repeated. "I look like a goddamn comedian?"

"No, but—"

"Then pay me some respect, okay? I'm an important man, I'm a big man. I need you, but you don't need me. So you're gonna give me what I need or you're not gonna get what you need. You know that and I know that, so let's not pussyfoot around. Let's just keep the action going, the ball in play, all right?"

He had no idea what half this shit meant but, hell, he was on a roll. Yeah, you better believe it.

Her voice starting to weaken, she said, "Mr. Fisher, I can't—"

Max dropped the headphones, got up and walked away. He went all the way to the other end of the room, making it seem like he was leaving for real, then, at the door, he stopped and turned back. Sure enough the book bitch was calling to him, trying to get his attention.

Max had her!

But he took his time walking back, milking the moment, then put the phones on and she practically screamed, "If I say yes, will you do the book with me?"

Ah, desperation. He loved it.

Max, waited, said, "Sweetheart, I'm gonna do a lot more with you than write a fucking book."

Max Fisher had to be the smarmiest, sleaziest, most self-deluded guy Paula had ever met—a goldmine all right. She'd been worried, on the way up to Attica, that maybe Fisher would be a disappointment. After all, how could a guy be so far out there, so far gone? But, no, this guy lived up to his rep and surpassed it.

Just arriving at Attica had been such a fucking blast.

The walls of the prison seemed to reek of testosterone and she'd laughed, said to herself, "Wanna talk about sperm count?"

She had to put that in the book. But first, Jesus, first, she needed to do another line. Yeah, just to get into the full Max Fisher mindset she'd started doing coke, and the sheer rush of snorting a line outside Attica was incredible. So she did one line, okay four, but c'mon, this is the toughest joint in the whole country and she was about to meet the craziest bastard any writer could dream of.

What was that book called, *The Journalist and the Murderer?* Yeah, something like that, Joe McGinnis, hottest true crime writer in the biz, two movies made till his subject, the killer doctor—McDonald?—sued him and sayonara Joe. Dealing with these guys was like juggling grenades. But if you could handle it…and she could, she knew she could. Now it was Paula Segal's turn in the spotlight, on center stage.

The coke kicking in, she took a sip of her stone-cold vanilla latte. (Decaf. She wasn't reckless. That caffeine was, like, addictive.)

She reached in her glove compartment, the nose candy giving her that icy drip that was pure heaven, and yup, there were her Virginia Slims. A cigarette, even a girly one, and she was so ready to rock and roll.

Oh, she loved Fisher. Who could invent a guy like that? She already had the chapter written in her head where he proposed marriage. Perfect, fucking perfect.

He hadn't been able to take his eyes off her tits. His

obsession with busty women had come up during his trial and, okay, she'd expected him to respond more or less the way he had. It's why she'd worn what she'd worn. But he'd gone further. Three weeks in jail and he was ready to propose marriage to a complete stranger. One with nice tits, but still. Couldn't this asshole tell she was a dyke now? But if he couldn't, he couldn't. Not her fault. It was her right as a journalist to milk it for all it was worth. She decided to string him along, let him think she wanted to marry him. Jesus, how far would a man go just to get laid? But if that's what it took to get him to open up in a few private sessions, give her some juicy quotes no one else had, baby, let him eye the twins all he wanted. About time they gave her something other than a backache.

Leaving the prison, Paula was shaking, not from fear but sheer hot exhilaration. Well, exhilaration and cocaine.

She did another line then, looking up at the gun turrets, realized she'd better get the car and her ass in gear.

As she pulled out of there, she was debating, Should she reveal in the book that she was gay? Then she thought, *How big is the pink dollar?* and laughed again, that damn coke. *How much did dykes spend on true crime books?*

But no, pulling an Ellen might alienate the great white majority. The hell with it, she'd ask her agent what to do, her *new* agent, not this fucking loser she had now.

Getting back to the motel, she found the coke high, like a sad dick, was wilting and she needed to stay up, stay on top of her game. She thought, *Nice cold dry Martini would do the biz, maybe a bit of hot sex. She'd check her trick book —*

But, shit, she wasn't in the city. Her trick book was back home, and anyone listed in it was three hundred miles away. She needed some rough trade right here, right now. There had to some hot bull dykes somewhere in Attica, New York, right? Every prison these days had a diversity hiring requirement, and those butch female guards had to hang out somewhere.

Her thoughts skipped back, from sex to her book. She could see the dust jacket, had to be black and white, maybe they'd use Fisher's mugshot. Or maybe she'd just take one herself, how difficult could it be? She had a digital camera.

Then the blurbs! Maybe she could get Dominick Dunne or Sebastian Junger or, better yet, Bill Clinton. He liked to read and, God, he was going to love to read about Max Fisher. Ah, and then, once word of her book got around, people would start asking *her* for blurbs, Even Connelly and King would be calling her. But she'd adopt a policy of *no blurbing* herself. Sorry, not even for Laura L.

She said aloud as she was putting on her leather gear, primed for a night on the prowl, something that would have gotten her thrown out of the very bars she was about to visit: "Max Fisher, I love you."

Eleven

*"Ehi, chi ha fascino puo permettersi
di camminare impettito, no?"*
KEN BRUEN AND JASON STARR, *Doppio Complotta*

Sebastian was so bloody happy to be back in old Blighty. Gosh, it was good to speak English with English people. He'd noticed the girl on the plane had spare keys in her bag and stupid cow, her address in Hampstead written right on the fob. Who knows, he might do a little reconnaissance there. He always kept his ears open for useful details. She'd mentioned she worked as a paralegal; perhaps while she was paralegalizing, he could stroll through her gaff, see what other goodies he might liberate.

The prospect of rifling her place tickled his fancy. Nothing like a touch of B-and-E to whet the appetites. He had for the past few years rented a one-room apartment in Earls Court. His parents paid the freight, mainly to keep him out of their home. Patrick Hamilton had written, "Those whom the gods have abandoned are left an electric fire in Earls Court." It was indeed, depending on your vocabulary,

A kip
A hovel
A dive
A shithole

But it was a bolt hole, and it was useful to have an address. It had one wardrobe that held his prized Armani suit, his three pair of Italian-made brogues and, of course, the mandatory striped shirts, all bespoke. And, naturally, an assortment of ties, from Police Federation to Cambridge, Eton and Oxford to the Masons. Vital items for a con man on his uppers.

He needed an infusion of cash, a rather large one. He took out his remaining bottle of Gordon's Gin—was there any other?—and drat, no tonic or bitters, really, he'd have to take stock. There was a miniature mountain of bills that had accumulated in his absence, and he threw them in the garbage. The upper classes didn't actually *pay* for stuff. Really, did anyone ever see Prince Charles worry about the light bill?

He tossed back the gin, said, "Hits the spot, ye gads."

And went to the bathroom. It was about the size of his cupboard. Shame about the hot water. There is a slight downside to not paying the utilities. He'd have to ring ol' Mum, get her to post some cheques to these various chappies. He splashed on some Hugo Boss, a fellow had to smell right, and then as he peed, he went, "The bloody hell is that?"

Couldn't be. But it looked like…were those *blisters*?

He stood stock still, thinking, Herpes? Him?

"The bitch," he said, and he slammed his fist into the wall, hurting his knuckles. Then he shouted, "This is just too *bloody rich!*"

And in his rage, he made a decision that, by day's end, would in fact lead to his killing somebody.

He went back to the tiny front room, drank off rather a large measure of neat gin and in a lightbulb moment thought, Hampstead, by golly. Somebody is going to pay for this injustice, this travesty of life.

He went to the pub first, see if any of the chaps were around, maybe hit them for a rapid fifty for cab fare. You didn't think he was going to ride the tube, now did you? Come on, really, get with the cricket, old bean.

The usual suspects were lined up along the bar and greeted him less with warmth than expectation, expecting that for once he might be flush and stand a round of drinks, they admired his tan, and when he shouted to the bartender, "Pint of your best bitter, my good fellow," they shrugged, collectively, same old, same old.

It was the kind of pub where everything was for sale, even your mother, well, your mother's pension, anyway. There was a quite a brisk trade in old age pensioners' pension books, and of course there was always someone cashing some unfortunate Australian backpacker's travelers cheques. You recommended a good cheap hostel to them, clean and friendly, and while they went off to make the call, you relieved them of their belongings.

Doing the chaps and gells a favour, actually. Now they'd really have an adventure, see how friendly

London was when you were skint. Which is why all the bar staff in Earls Court had Aussie accents, the trips to Italy, etc., shall we say, um, deferred.

Sebastian managed to bum a twenty from an Irish guy who was three sheets to the wind and got the hell out of there. The black cab to Hampstead cost most of the borrowed dosh but ah, glorious Hampstead, where Sebastian felt he belonged—that, or of course, Windsor.

He paid the driver and gazed in wonder at the address. It was a semi-detached in a nice leafy lane. Whistling a few bars from *Bridge on the River Kwai*, he let himself in, hoping to fuck she didn't have a dog.

Cash, the house reeked of it. Flokati shag rugs on the floor and paintings, dammit all, one of them looked like a, golly gosh, *a Constable.* And the decoration, even to his untrained eye, had obviously cost a bundle, all that posh leather furniture that creaked when you sat in it but looked good in the glossy mags. First things first, he found the drinks cabinet, found, ah yes, Gordon's and mixers. Then he found a nice large Gucci holdall and began to fill it with swag.

Then upstairs and women, ha, so predictable. Under her rather dainty lingerie he found nigh on five large in notes and nearly had a coronary when he found, in a leather pouch, a roll of Krugerrands, with a note:

Love from Daddykins
Xxxxx

He was toasting Daddykins when a voice asked, "Who the hell are you?"

Turned to see a woman in her fifties, with a cleaning brush and apron. He was startled, then tried, "Golly, one wasn't expecting the char to arrive."

For the life of him, he couldn't remember the name of the bloody cow who lived here. Meanwhile, the cleaning woman was like all her class, suspicious, and accused, "You're a burglar."

In his agitation, he thought she called him a *bugger*. Now I mean, steady on, a chap had some horseplay with the rugger boys in boarding school, it was part of being English, but to be actually called a homo…

She picked up the phone near the bed, said, "I'm calling the coppers."

A combination of herpes shock, bugger accusation, gin, and *Ripley's Game* meshed and he had the phone cord round her neck in no time. She fought like a demon, they fell over the bed, but he held on for grim life and even began to laugh hysterically, shouting, "Ride 'em, cowboy!"

Took a time and she managed to scrape his face, hurt like a…a bugger? The cord was near embedded in her throat when she finally gave out and went limp.

He was shaking, rose off her. He got all his loot together, too drunk to realize his prints were all over the place. He didn't dare call a cab, so he legged it down the leafy lane, found a tube station and, loath as he was to use that service, he did. On the train, a wino asked him for a contribution and he answered, "Bugger off."

When he finally got to Earls Court, he was seriously knackered, the adrenaline long gone, and his hangover had kicked in with a serious intent. Probably explains why he didn't notice his door had been forced. He just wanted to have a shower and count the loot and oh, have a large gin. Killing people was harder work than they led you to believe. He'd done it twice, and you know, it didn't get easier.

He was reaching for the light switch when he got a massive wallop to the head that sent him sprawling across his tiny living room, the bag of swag spilling every which way, a rainbow of miniature paintings, jewelry, Krugerrands, cash, a few pair of the girl's lace panties he'd grabbed, even one of the flokati rugs.

He turned to see Georgios standing over him. Georgios, how the fuck could that be? The guy was fish meat off the cliffs of Santorini. Jesus, how rough was his hangover? Hallucinating already?

Georgios hissed, "I'm going to cut your balls off, mallakas, for the death of my cousin."

Good to his word, he had a very lethal looking knife in his right hand. Sebastian held up a hand, asked, "You're his cousin?"

He didn't know whether to feel relief or fear. He ranted, "I tried to *save* Georgios. It was that crazy American bitch killed him. Why do you think I left her behind? She's completely mad."

The knife was raised, and Sebastian had an inspiration that saved his balls and his life.

He said, "See all this treasure, we can use it to track her down, extract proper vengeance for your noble cousin."

Noble certainly stopped the mad bastard in his knife tracks. He asked, "Why should I believe you, mallakas?"

Sebastian was on his feet now, grabbed the gin bottle, poured two large measures and, with a shaking hand, offered it to the guy, who grabbed it, tried it, made a face. Sebastian knocked his back like a drowning man, said, "I was living on Santorini for months, I never even heard of your noble cousin, why would I kill him? But this crazy woman, she owed him rent, she stole from me, she is truly demented."

The guy had put the knife down, thank God, and was looking at all the cash and goodies lying on the floor.

Sebastian quickly added, the gin urging him on, "My parents are rich and this is my inheritance."

Why they would have given him some rather delicate items of lingerie was tricky but the Greeks knew all about the, um, peccadillos of the Brits.

The guy said, "I found your credit card in Georgios' home."

Dammit, must've fallen out of his pocket while he was bending over, wrapping the body in plastic.

Fucking credit cards, always came back to bite you in the bum.

The Greek pushed his glass towards Sebastian, grunted, "More."

Sebastian thought, the scoundrel might have tried *please*. But this was probably not the best moment to mention it.

The man said, "My name is Yanni."

Would *Damn jolly good to meet you* be overdoing it? Sebastian settled for, "Glad to meet you. Alas, I wish it were under happier circumstances, but be assured, I will track this lady down and wreak revenge for you and your family."

He was thinking, give the bastard five hundred for his trouble and get shot of him. Well, let's not be rash, two hundred was probably a fortune to a chappie like this.

The guy had rock-hard eyes, said, "We."

Sebastian echoed, "We?…I'm not sure I follow you, old chap."

Yanni was looking at the knife again, said, "I don't trust you English, we stay together till this is avenged, okay?"

With a sinking heart, Sebastian mustered his best grin, said, "Splendid, rather chuffed to have you on board."

Yanni grabbed a pile of cash and Sebastian thought, *Steady on*.

The Greek was heading for the door, said, "Now

we eat, drink some ouzo, and plan how we find this she-devil."

Sebastian wanted a shower and more gin and to be rid of this lunatic.

"Capital," he said.

Twelve

Dyke City

If there was a dyke scene in Attica, New York, Paula Segal sure as hell was going to find it. She did a couple of lines of coke on the dashboard, made sure her push-up bra was doing its necessary pushing up, and was ready to roll.

She drove to downtown Attica and a good thing she didn't blink too long or she would've missed it. It was the typical small upstate New York town that had been thriving during the time they filmed *It's a Wonderful Life* but now it looked like a ghost town, probably the casualty of a nearby Wal-Mart. But the lesbians had to hang out somewhere, right? She drove by a few dilapidated blocks, past the mostly abandoned shops. There were a few bars, but only one getting any business. As she entered, Kiss' "Rock And Roll All Night" was blasting. She had a feeling this wasn't a good sign.

The place was crowded, that was the good news. The bad news was the ratio was bad, i.e. there were practically all men. Standing in the doorway, Paula felt the sets of male eyes leering at her desperately, as if she was the first woman they'd seen in years. Jeez, was the whole town of Attica a freaking prison? Did they release them right into the goddamn bars?

One guy grabbed her arm—he looked frighteningly like Sean Penn in *Dead Man Walking*—and said, "Hey, how about a little dance, honey?"

Like you could dance to Kiss.

She yanked her arm free, hissed, "Fuck you, townie."

God, men were so fucking gross. Did she actually used to like them or had she gone through the eighteen years of her sexually active life faking it? Eh, whatever, she was just so glad she was through with all of that crap.

The woman working the bar—she wasn't bad looking. Blond, a little heavy but, hey, Paula liked big girls. The woman looked briefly in Paula's direction and half-smiled, but Paula couldn't tell if there was more to it, if it was a come-on or not. As a newbie lesbian, Paula's gaydar wasn't fully developed yet. Since she'd, well, *turned*, she'd accidentally hit on several straight women and she was sure she'd let some hardcore dykes, easy lays, slip through her fingers. She hoped it all averaged out in the end.

Paula sat at the bar and decided to go native, ordered a bottle of Schlitz.

Watching the woman get the drink, Paula eyeballed her ass. Nice. She liked her shoulders, too—they were big and meaty. She had at least a few tattoos, wasn't wearing makeup, and her hair was cut short, boyish. Looked like a dyke all right.

"Hey, I'm Paula."

"Bonny," the woman said.

Paula smiled, said, "Shake your bon-bon, shake your bon-bon."

Bonny was deadpan. Maybe she didn't like Ricky Martin?

Trying to loosen her up, Paula said, "It's kinda guy-heavy here tonight, huh?"

"Yeah," Bonny said, "but this is the clientele. What're you gonna do, you know?"

"I know what *I'm* gonna do," Paula said.

She smiled, letting the implication linger, as if there was any doubt what she had in mind.

"Excuse me, are you hitting on me?" Bonny asked.

She seemed if not disgusted, seriously annoyed.

Before Paula could respond a fat guy with a scraggly red beard appeared.

He said, "What's the problem, honey?

"This lady's hitting on me," Bonny said.

Paula said, "Um, I think there's a, um, misunder—"

"You tryin' to pick up my wife?" Bearded Guy asked.

Somebody in the bar yelled, "She's a fuckin' dyke!" and then everybody started yelling.

Paula hightailed it out of there, back to her car. As she was getting in, Bearded Guy came running over, saying, "Hey, if you're lookin' to have one of 'em three-somes, maybe I can talk Bonny into it!"

Back in her motel room, Paula got undressed and into bed, thinking, So much for hooking up in this hick town. She read a few chapters of Lippman's *What the Dead Know*, then on pay-per-view she found a good

all-girl porno movie—*Horny College Chicks Get Dirty*.
As the girls went at it, wrestling and clawing at each
other in the mud, she moved her hand over her crotch,
whispering, "That'll do, pig. That'll do."

In the morning, Paula left bright and early for her first
session with Max.

The warden had come through, and she found herself sitting face-to-face next to Fisher, a guard near the
door. Fisher was, naturally, staring at her bust.

After last night the last thing she was in the mood
for was a predatory man. But she reminded herself
that her career was at stake and she had to put on her
game face.

Fisher asked, "So you wanna set a date?

She stared at him. She didn't know what he was
talking about, said, "What're you talking about?"

"Tomorrow my morning's full," he said, "but how
about the afternoon?"

Talk about gaydar malfunctioning, what was wrong
with this guy?

"I'm sorry, a date for what?"

"Our fucking wedding," he said. "The M.A.X. needs
to get his pipes cleaned. I already got permission from
my counselor and last night I wrote out a pre-nup. It
basically says, You don't get shit. Sorry to be so blunt
about it but, hey, I learned from the Donald. I know
it's probably not legally binding, but it'll give me something to fall back on when our marriage goes to pieces
and, let's face it, I know it's gonna feel like a honey-

moon now, but it's only a matter of time before it all goes to shit. Trust me, when it comes to shit relationships I've been there, done that."

Trying not to laugh, she said, "This is all so sudden. I need some more time to think about it."

Fisher wouldn't crack. He said, "I need an answer pronto. No marry, no talkie. You have ten seconds to decide."

He started the countdown and she was thinking how she couldn't lose this book deal. But marry Fisher? God, he made Ron Jeremy look like a catch. But if she had to do it, she had to do it. This was her last shot and she wasn't giving it up for anything.

He was at "two" when she blurted, "Yes, yes, I'll marry you, I'll marry you."

Fisher leaned over and, Jesus Christ, he kissed her. Cringing, she was thinking of that line from *Planet of the Apes* when Dr. Zira kisses Charlton Heston: *You're so damn ugly*.

She couldn't wait to get out of there, to take a shower, but she reminded herself of her ultimate goal, to write the best damn true crime book ever, and she tried to keep her disgust from showing.

Max was talking about the marriage license and setting a date for sometime next week. Hopefully she'd have all the material she needed by then and wouldn't have to go through with it.

Speaking of which. She said, "Tell more about this hit man you and Angela Petrakos allegedly hired to kill your wife. Did he really call himself Popeye?"

It spread like wildfire that The M.A.X. had had a *hot* visitor.

One guy asked, "That, like, your wife?"

Max gave him a withering look, sneered, "Ain't you heard, peckerhead? My first bitch wife got chopped to pieces." Let the other cons hear this as he paused. Added a wink, then said, "By person or persons unknown."

They could check this out and see indeed it was true. It should further enhance his violent rep.

The guy took off, muttering, "No offense, bro."

Man, Max was having the time of his freaking life. Did he own this joint or what? Even the guards were looking at him with fresh respect. And the writer babe, the bust on that chick! He was hard just replaying the scene and the way he'd laid down the rules to her. He could see she was panting for him, he knew all about how those crazy dames married guys in the joint. Soon he'd have a stack of letters from women wanting to be his penpal. The M.A.X. might allow one of the queens to do his letter writing, they were good at all that romance shit.

Another con stopped, asked, "Mr. Max, you need me to run any errands, stuff like that?"

Max gave him his imperial look, said, "I seem to be running low on decent booze."

Let it hover.

The guy, some variety of spic, licked his lips, said, "There's the prison hooch, I can get you a bottle of that." Trailed off as The M.A.X. gave him the silent treatment then said, "There's a bottle of Chivas going for like five cartons."

Max gave him a tiny pat on the shoulder, said, "Now you're talking, *hermano*, deliver it to my cell in say, ten minutes?"

When Max finally got back to the cell, Rufus was standing there, gazing in wonder at a bottle of Chivas, said, "You the man, yo, how the hell you get this shit? How much it gonna cost?"

Rufus, who knew how the system worked, had never even seen real booze in all his years in lockup. Max smiled, took the bottle, said, "I let him live."

Max clinked his prison-issue tin cup again Rufus's. Chivas in a tin cup. Thought to himself, Hmmmm, maybe a good title for the book of poetry he'd been thinking he might write someday. He was just so on fire. Then he laughed to himself and said out loud, "I'm a fucking riot." Later, he'd remember saying this, after he'd become the cause of one of the bloodiest fucking riots to come down the pike. Wouldn't seem so funny then, but for now he couldn't stop chuckling.

He had another shot of the Chivas, man, that was good shit, he didn't know if the big guy appreciated the finer things in life but hey, hang in there, The M.A.X. would bring him right along. He reminded Max of the giant in *The Green Mile*, and he made a metal note, tell the writer babe to put ol' Rufus in there.

Then he realized the big guy was...*sobbing?* The fuck was that? How good was this booze?

Max, allowing his sensitive side to show, asked, "Hey, *amigo mio*, whassup?"

Then to keep his Spanish in trim, added, *"Que pasa, compadre?"*

Rufus, massive tears rolling down those cheeks, said, "Yo, Max, man, I just been feeling so bad and shit, know what I'm sayin'? When you came in here, me wantin' to ram a rod up yo' pretty ass and shit? That shit was wrong, know what I'm sayin'? That shit wasn't me talkin', man, you gotta know that shit's true." He sobbed some more, then said, "Outside, man, I never even been lookin' at another man's ass, know what I'm sayin'? But inside here, shit, it fucks with a man's mind and shit. You see the sissies walkin' 'round shakin' they pretty asses and you start wantin' some of that shit yourself, know what I'm sayin'? You start sayin', 'Gimme some a dat shit,' 'I want some a dat shit.' 'I wanna fuck that shit.' Know what I'm sayin'?" He wiped his eyes on the back of his hand. "And, Max, yo, if I been knowin' you was some hot shit gangsta an' shit, I wouda been cleanin' yo' ass fer you every day 'stead a wantin' to fuck it, know what I'm sayin'? Why would I would I wanna fuck some big time gangsta's ass for? That's shit's crazy, man, shit makes no sense and shit. And some a the shit I been sayin' to you, man, like how I been hatin' Moslems and shit, I didn't mean none of that shit. I don't know why I said that 'cept I was crazy cause I been in this jail too long and I been gettin' too much sissy ass. It fucks with a man's brain and shit, know what I'm sayin'? And now, every night, I been afraid. Yeah, I been afraid that I wake up my dick won' be on my body no more. Every night, 'fore I go to sleep I pray to Jesus you won't take off my dick. And every mornin' when I wake up, first thing I do is I check to make sure my dick's still there. So that's what I'm sayin' to you is thank you, man. Thank you for not takin' my dick off, and I hope you forgive me for disrespectin' you and shit. I didn't mean none of that shit. That was just bullshit talkin', that wasn't me."

Man, Max was soaking all this up, he didn't want it to stop. He knew moments like this, they didn't come along too often in life and he had to milk it for all it was worth. He had this huge terrifying black cellmate, a serious gangsta who could crush him with one hand, and not only was the man living his life in total fear of Max, he was also begging for his forgiveness. He glared at Rufus hard for a long time, as if he were weighing all his options.

Then, expansive and like the Mahatma, forgiving like Gandhi but with a shitload of Chivas on board, Max finally said, "*De nada, señor*. Ain't no big thang."

Whoops, how did he go Texan? Eh, what the fuck ever. He was forgiving the mutherfucka, not forgetting, or as Dr. Phil might say, *Moving on and moving up*.

But Rufus kept talking and truth to tell, it was grating just a tiny tad on Max's nerves. He was about to snap when Rufus blurted out, "I got a secret, man."

Max, in his most humble, quiet voice, said, "Pray tell?"

Which reminded him, he better get that preacher validation on the web, 100 bucks and you were like, *An ordained preacher of the church of outreach saints*. Two fags on the upper tier wanted to get hitched and he'd told them for four hundred bucks he would perform the ceremony. Was there truly no end to his talents? Prison was ripe, fucking abundant in business opportunities. Ask that Watergate guy, Colson.

He had to refocus. Rufus was spilling, "We got a break comin'."

Max, muddled by the Chivas and his myriad schemes and languages, thought first he meant someone was, like, going to cut them a bit of slack, then he realized, *prison break*. Sweet Jesus, like the TV series. This would put the book up there with Dan Brown. Wait till Paula heard about this. It would have to at least get him a great blowjob, right?

Rufus was saying, "Yo, I only trustin you cause you a gangsta and I got respect for you an' shit. I ain't even tol' the rest of my crew, but you the man, Max Fisher, know what I'm sayin'? We been plannin' this shit for three years. And we ain't stupid and shit neither. We're gonna do this shit up right, know what I'm sayin'? Now we got a gangsta like you on our side, shit, we're gonna be all set up. So you wanna be in, you just say the word and you in, know what I'm sayin'?"

Max waited, trying his hardest to stay stone-faced, to put the fear of God in his cellmate, then asked, "When y'all gonna make your move?"

"When them riots come down," Rufus said, "know

what I'm sayin'? Everybody be fightin' and shit and we be sneakin' our asses outta this jail. Damn, I can't wait to get outside an jam my dick into some real pussy, know what I'm sayin'? Man, I been fuckin' so many sissies' asses I don't even 'member what real pussy feel like."

Max was thinking: Riots, a prison break, Hollywood, fame. Was he the luckiest guy on the planet or what?

"Count me in, baby," he nearly shouted.

Thirteen

*"All day long I experienced infinite sadness amid grey
surroundings. I collected one by one my sullied hopes,
and I cried over each of them."*
ANDRE GIDE, *The White Notebook*

Manhattan used to give Angela a big buzz, but not
anymore. The city had disappointed her so many times
that arriving in midtown and being in the center of it
all once again left her feeling depressed more than
anything else. It reminded her of all the failures, all
her disappointments, all her dreams gone to shite. She
couldn't even muster up a fantasy that this time around
things would work out differently. Why should they?

Her cash was running so low—maybe that gift to
the British girl on the ferry hadn't been the smartest
move in the world—that she couldn't afford a cab and
had to take a bus into the city. A hotel was out of the
question, so it was either Max Fisher or bust. She had
no idea if he'd take her back, but she was out of
options. If this didn't work she might have to sleep on
the street tonight, or on the subway.

She took the 6 train uptown and headed over to the
apartment building on the Upper East Side where
she'd spotted him briefly the last time she was in the
city. In a strange way she was looking forward to

seeing him again. Yeah, he was bonkers and sleazy, but she wasn't exactly the portrait of mental health and fidelity her own self. Maybe they were destined to be together—two tortured souls who'd been around the block more than a few times and who, in the end, realize they're perfect for each other. You could even see something romantic about it, if you squinted.

She went to the concierge desk. The guy was on the phone and Angela looked around, impressed with the décor in the lobby. Jaysus, Max was probably rolling in it. Before she'd left for Greece, she'd read in the paper how he'd become a drug dealer, and she knew he must have been doing well at it, to live in a swank building on the Upper East Side. But she'd had no idea he'd been doing *this* well. Too bad she didn't look her best after the long flight, the ferry ride to Athens and the, well, encounter in the Greek prison. She knew a first impression was everything and she wanted Max to see her in her best light. But then she expanded her chest and looked down proudly, remembering that with Max these babies were all she'd ever needed.

The concierge finished the call and Angela said, "I'm here to see Max Fisher."

The guy nearly laughed, said, "He doesn't live here anymore."

"Oh, okay, do you know where he's living now?"

"Yeah, Attica."

Angela was still lost in her daydream, imagining living off of Max's millions, straightening out her life once and for all. She figured, Attica, that must be the name of some luxury condo: The Attica. Yeah, it was probably right next door to Trump Tower or something.

"Is that on the Upper East Side, too?" she asked hopefully.

The guy laughed again, said, "It's a jail, honey. You know in upstate New York? He got sent away. You didn't hear about it? He left owing three months rent. Cheap son of a bitch never tipped me, not once… You're not a relative, are you?"

She didn't answer, just walked away.

She should've known. Wasn't it always the way? Whenever she had the slightest hope that things might work out for her after all, fate always snuck up on her and kicked her in the ass.

She went outside and naturally it had started to rain. Pushing her suitcase ahead of her, the rain pouring down on her, she walked across town to the Port Authority bus terminal and spent the last of her money on a one-way ticket to Attica.

The bus didn't leave till five a.m. so Angela had to spend the night in the terminal. The saddest thing was no one even tried to pick her up.

When she was a teenager, living with her parents in Weehawken, New Jersey, she took buses into the city all the time and guys at the Port Authority always hit on her. Once, when she was seventeen a guy in a leather vest with a handlebar mustache approached her and asked her if she was interested in becoming a model. She was so naïve then she actually thought it was a good career opportunity, that she'd been discovered. So they went to his "studio"—it didn't ever occur to her to ask why a photographer would have his studio in a practically condemned S.R.O. in Hell's Kitchen— and after a few minutes of general-type questions he asked her to take her clothes off. She thought this was a little, well, unusual, but he explained that all the girls did it and if she wanted to make a thousand bucks a week she'd have to take nude modeling gigs.

She knew where this was leading and asked, "Wait, so are you, like, a porno director?"

"I make adult films, yes," he said.

She couldn't figure out if she was offended or flattered. She knew she should be offended, but it was kind of exciting, the thought of getting into the adult entertainment business. And, hey, she could be the next Jenna Jameson.

So she took off her shirt and undid her bra, waiting for the admiration to begin. But when the guy got a look at her barely A-cup breasts he said, "Sorry, no thanks," and practically kicked her out of the place.

She hadn't thought much of it at the time, she'd just been pissed off; but if there was a life-changing moment in Angela's life, that had been it. The rejection by the porno director had led to a downward spiral. Several years later she took the Pam Anderson/Anna Nicole Smith route and got her boobs done and went blonde and even started wearing the blue contacts. She barely looked like her old self. But had her new look made her any happier? Had it fuck. For years her body had sent out the wrong signals, attracted the worst possible men, and what was it doing for her now? Men were walking by her, ignoring her, like she was fooking invisible. If you couldn't get a guy to notice you at the Port Authority you knew you were way past your sell-by date.

Finally, she got on the bus and, unable to sleep, stared blankly out the window. If she'd been in a less hopeless state she might have realized that there wasn't much point in spending the last of her money to go visit Max. After all, how would a guy serving a stiff jail sentence, who was apparently broke when he got sent up and whose life had clearly gone down the shitter, be able to help her? In her desperation, she was hoping that Max had stashed some money away and would help her out for old time's sake. Yeah, okay, their relationship hadn't always been great and she'd nearly gotten him killed a couple of times, but it hadn't been all bad. There had been times when she felt close to him, when she'd actually enjoyed his company. Okay, maybe she was just imagining this, but he was certainly the wisest man she'd ever known. All right, maybe that wasn't saying much given her dating history. But despite all his shortcomings, there was no doubt that he was a sharp guy, right? He'd built a business and become a self-made millionaire. You can't pull that off and be a total idiot, can you? He also seemed to have made quite a splash as a drug dealer, showed that the first time wasn't just a stroke of luck. He was also in touch with himself, always meditating and talking about Buddhist shite. Maybe at the very least he could advise her, tell her what to do to straighten her life out.

When she arrived in Attica, she was exhausted, had barely slept in forty-eight hours. Still, she was focused and went right to a drugstore. Her checkered history had taught her some things like check out for CCTV. Nope, nothing she could see, so she helped herself to some Chanel. Max had always been partial to his lady smelling fine. Then she went down the block to a thrift shop. The owner was absorbed, reading a copy of the local pennysaver, so she went to the back and boosted a dress, low cut to let that cleavage show, and though hardly cutting-edge fashion, it was clean and bright. She already had her heels, never left home without them.

Good to go, she left the store, her mood slightly elevated. It was a rush to shoplift right under the shadow of one of the country's most notorious prisons. It lifted her confidence, showed she still had some moves, and she felt she was going to need them.

She hitched a ride to the prison. Wasn't hard—seemed like everyone was heading in that direction. It was apparently the big attraction in town, like freaking Disneyland.

She hadn't inquired about visiting hours and she found out she needed to arrange her visit in advance. No problem there though—a little flirting with the guard got her through, the stolen dress already paying some dividends.

She was in the visitor's room, waiting for Max to appear. She expected Max to shuffle in looking beaten, defeated and lost. Older guy like him, not exactly athletic, they'd have eaten him alive by now. She figured she'd give him a dose of sympathy, a little TLC, and that might shake the bucks loose from him.

Her first surprise was when he was led into the room, was she imagining it or was the guard acting all deferential? And Max, glowing with well-being and satisfaction, a smile of utter confidence on his face. He looked like he'd been on a health farm for months. Even looked like he'd lost a few pounds.

He motioned to the guard, and Angela could read his lips: *I'll call you if I need you, Bob*.

Dismissing him? The fook was this?

He sat, stared at her deadpan for a while, then said, "So what's shaking, babe?"

Total strut, acting like he didn't miss her at all, like he might've even forgotten she existed.

She said, "I heard you were here and I was concerned and thought I better come and see if you needed anything."

He gave his high-pitched laugh, the one that had always grated on her nerves. But she hid her distaste, knowing pissing him off wouldn't accomplish anything. Naturally he was staring at her tits.

"Them the same babies I paid serious green for?"

Actually, she'd paid for her own boob job, but if he wanted to believe they were his, why bust his bubble?

She tried to look coy, been a long time since she'd had to use that gig, said, "All yours, hon."

Jesus, she could tell it was killing him, he was dying to come around, cop a feel. Instead, he sat back, yawned. Fucking yawned. Was she, like, boring him?

He asked, "So, my treacherous bitch, what's the real reason you're here? Last time I saw you, you were putting it to me big time—and not your first shafting of The M.A.X. either."

The M.A.X.?

She tried to stay coy, not easy, said, "We all got bent a little out of shape back in those crazy days but I realize now, I'll never meet a man like you again."

Prick bought it. Always did.

He said, "You got The M.A.X., you don't need nothin' else, dig?"

Christ, how could she have forgotten what a dumb arrogant bollix he was?

Poverty will do that, make you stupid. But here she was and all out of options. She said, "I thought we might start over."

He stared at her, said, "You're broke."

Not so dumb.

She said, "Well, I won't lie to you. Things have been a little tight."

"And you coming to The M.A.X., cause he like yo' fixer and shit, right?"

God, was he for real? There'd never been a white man whiter than Max Fisher, and here he was talking like some kind of rapper.

He spread his arm out, said, "See that yard out there, with the most dangerous dudes on the planet? I run 'em, run 'em like the fuckin' losers they are."

How, she asked herself, had someone not gutted the little bastard already? And how on earth did he manage to become top rooster in such a place?

"You always were extraordinary," she said, and wanted to throw up.

He leaned over, said, "Gonna share a secret with you babe, the joint ain't been built that can hold The M.A.X."

Jaysus, he was completely mad.

He continued, "We're busting outa here, me and my crew."

She didn't know how to respond, tried lamely, "That's wonderful."

He smiled, accepting the praise as his due, said, "You want back with The M.A.X., you gonna have to prove your loyalty."

She said, getting the faint whiff of money, and remembering how if she didn't hook up with somebody tonight she'd be sleeping on the street.

"You name it darling, it's done."

He scribbled something onto a piece of paper, then slid it across and said, "Get it done."

She looked down. He'd written two words:

GUNS

CAR

She didn't have bus fare back to the city and he wanted her to get him guns? Never mind a *car*.

She nearly laughed till he reached in his denim shirt, took out a roll of bills, said. "To get you started. And oh, get some decent clothes, that dress looks like it came from fucking Goodwill."

Then he was standing and did cop a feel, a long one. She moaned. He mistook it for a sound of pleasure.

He said, "Go get your pretty ass in gear. Sooner you get me out of here, the sooner The M.A.X. will be putting the meat to you."

Then he shouted for Bob, winked at her, said, "Don't fuck up this time, bee-otch, you know what I'm sayin'?"

Fourteen

"Hop smiled. 'Nice, could you run my life, baby?'
'Some challenges are too great, my friend.' "
MEGAN ABBOTT, *The Song is You*

Max couldn't believe it—Angela was fucking back! He'd had to contain himself because, hey, that's the way you had to play it in the joint. Max had done his DD, studying the bros in yard, and almost all of them had the dead-eye glare. Not a lot of smiling faces in a maximum security prison and he knew if you wanted to survive you had to look hard, be hard, always have your game face on. Besides, it was part of Max's hip-hop persona. Look at Eminem. If Slim Shady didn't smile, Max sure as fuck wasn't going to.

But Jesus Christ, Angela looked fucking hot! Her bust, shit, it brought back so many great memories. Fuck, even her stretch marks looked hot. But what was up with that cheap dress? You wouldn't see a crack whore on the West Side Highway in something like that. And she was nervous, too, not the confident, cocky Angela who'd screwed him over so many times before. She looked a little shocked—scratch that, way shocked. Hell, she looked defeated. Angela, down and out? The fuck did that happen? The Angela he knew never stopped fighting. No matter what shit came down the road, she was there, scratching and biting like an alley cat, mouthing like a fishwife on steroids, and screwing the world. She'd ripped him off and just about every other dumb bastard whose path she'd crossed, but she'd never *caved,* no siree.

Suddenly Max found himself feeling like he was wasting his time with Paula. Yeah, the girl had a nice rack, and there was her book—but come on, there was no way he was gonna marry that cow if he could have Angela, the real deal. He and Angela were, like, *destined* to be together. Okay, yeah, so she'd tried to kill him a few times, but doesn't all true love go through rough patches? He'd bet there were times when Cleopatra had been more than a bit pissed off with Tony. And Romeo and Juliet probably wanted to scratch each other's fucking eyes out. Him and Angela, they were like Bonnie and Clyde—maybe occasionally too fast on the trigger, but still, together for life.

Yeah, Max wanted Angela, he wanted her bad. He wanted to cop a real good feel of that rack, too, but he had to see what she wanted first. Naturally it was money but, hey, he couldn't exactly blame her for that. Max had always been her Mr. Moneybags, her go-to guy for the green. And, he had to admit, her desperation was more than a bit of a turn-on for him. He didn't know what she'd done to fuck up her life this time but it must have been something big, maybe the biggest yet, because she was clearly at the end of her tether. Man, Max loved playing this role—Max Fisher the hero, Super Max swooping down to save the day.

But he wasn't going to bail out the psycho bitch just for the hell of it. His mind was working double-time—when wasn't it, right?—and he was thinking, How could he use this? Yeah, Rufus had invited him in on the break, but Max always liked to have a Plan B. Come on, let's face it, Rufus didn't have all the seeds in his apple. He probably had one-tenth or, hell, one hundredth the intellect of The M.A.X. Rufus had claimed some friend of his, some fucking gangbanger, would be waiting in a getaway car after the break, but did Max want to gamble his life on that? Fuck, Max had always been the Big Boss; he wasn't exactly comfortable letting some street thug he hadn't even met call the shots.

Which was why he'd slipped Angela a note to get weapons and a car. Knew he could trust the bitch as long as he was the one paying her. He figured he'd hit her with more instructions the next time he saw her. And, oh yeah, he knew she'd be back. Show Angela some moolah with the promise of more to come and you'd hooked her for life. It was what he loved about her. That, of course, and her tits.

Leaving the visitor's room, Max headed back to his cell. Sino was due to return from the hole tonight and, for the first time, Max caught a whiff of the riot in the air. It was a certain tension you could almost reach out and touch. Everyone was being ultra-careful, keeping their faces down and avoiding eye contact. The gangs were huddled together and the guards, the bulls, were way nervous. Tooling up, yeah, that was it. The gangs were stockpiling, shivs, crowbars, acid in bottles, you get that shit thrown in your face, that's all she wrote. Plywood was disappearing from the woodshop and clubs were being honed for maximum damage.

Max was getting a little concerned. All the talk about riots was cool and everything when it was all talk, but now it was getting a little too real, too imminent. But he psyched himself back up, telling himself he had the white supremacists all in his corner, plus Rufus. No one was gonna let The M.A.X. get hurt.

Straddling both sides, playing the middle, that was the way to go.

Rufus told him their homies had some serious armament ready to roll and even though some of them muttered about the white boy being part of the crew, Rufus slapped them down.

To sweeten the pie, Max had told him, "My main man, we get out of here, I'm going to set you up in a penthouse, lots of white meat and all the white powder you could stuff up that massive nose."

But the Crips, that was a different story.

Rufus said, "That Sino, he got a hard-on for yo' ass, boss. He get out, he gonna try to waste yo' ass in the craziness and shit."

That worried Max a little till Rufus said, "No worries my man, they let him out, Sino gonna be washing his brown ass in de shower and, shit, I settle his jones right there."

Meanwhile, Rufus finally filled him in on the

escape plan. It was so shot full of holes, Max couldn't believe it. In the smoke and mayhem of the riot, Rufus and crew were gonna hijack a laundry van and just mosey on out the main gate before full lockdown happened. They already had the uniforms, hidden away in a corner of the laundry room.

Could work, maybe, but Max was amazed. This was the plan they'd be working on for years? Max had figured they'd have a tunnel, a guy working on the inside, *something*. But he didn't want to ruin the party by bringing up any, like, doubts. Besides, he figured sometimes you did better going with something so basic, so crude, no one would ever imagine you'd try it.

When Rufus asked, "Boss, can you handle hardware, yo?" Max nearly sneered. He was the guy who'd emptied a full clip into the meanest muthahs you'd ever meet. Yeah, he could handle hardware, yo. He told Rufus all about the Colombians he'd smoked that time in Queens. Actually, he'd only shot one guy, and it had been a wild lucky shot, but like a fish story it got bigger with each telling. In the latest incarnation he'd smoked three sick-asses all packing serious heat.

Max went, "Get me a Mach 10, it's like my weapon of choice."

Rufus stared again at this stone cold killer, said, "Sound like you good to go, boss."

The Crips started the first step in what would be an out-and-out conflagration, burning their mattresses, taking a bull hostage. Later, the white supremacists cornered Max in the canteen. The leader, Arma, sitting Max down at his table, asked, "What's the deal, dude?"

Max, delighted to be called dude, said, "Ready to rumble."

"Ready? Man, it's already started. The Crips are burning mattresses, getting everything riled up, and they're coming for you first."

Max, terrified but not showing it, said, "I guess we'll just have to go medieval on their inferior asses."

Arma asked, "Their top guy, that Sino, how good is he?"

Max gave his superior laugh, made a show of looking at his watch, said, "About now, he's having the last shower of his life, he's going *clean* down the drain. One of my boys is helping him soap up as we speak."

Arma was impressed, said, "I'm impressed." Then he said, "But speaking of your boys…the niggers…*my* boys are a little concerned how much you're hanging with them."

Max leaned over, whispered, "They're gonna burn, and you my man, you're gonna own this joint."

He stifled a chuckle, thinking, *What's left of the fucking place*.

Arma said, "You're one cold cracker."

Max, standing, said, "You ain't seen nothing yet, dude."

Left him with his mouth hanging open.

Fifteen

"There's an armor the city makes you wear and look at him
defenseless, helmet dropped back blocks ago, no arm among
enemies strong enough to string the arrow that could pierce
his skin, rendering all cowards. Let us bow. No one bows."
COLSON WHITEHEAD, *The Colossus of New York*

Sebastian was in New York. He did not want to be in
fucking New York and he certainly did not want to be
in New York with a homicidal Greek who smelled of
olive oil all the time.

Yanni had never once let him out of his sight and
two days after their first meeting had bought tickets to
America, saying, "We get this done now."

Sebastian was seriously afraid of the maniac. If he
had demurred, he was sure the crazy bugger would
have slit his throat. He tried to look on the bright side,
maybe they would score some serious dosh off Angela.
Assuming they could ever find her.

What did irritate Sebastian a tad—well, ok, a lot—
was that Sebastian was paying the freight. Yanni had
disappeared with the biggest of the paintings; it had
turned out to be the real deal, a bloody *Constable*, and
he'd promptly fenced it. He'd flung ten large at
Sebastian and said, "Your share."

Was he going to argue that the scoundrel had probably gotten a damn fortune for it, hell of a lot more than twenty K? He took the cash, and talk about damn cheek, Yanni made Sebastian pay for the tickets, in business class no less. Put a hell of a dent in the ten.

Yanni carried on scandalously on the plane, drinking champagne like it was water, leering at the hostesses and, when the in-flight movie came on, something starring Nicole Kidman, he kept nudging Sebastian and making lewd comments. Sebastian tried to act like he wasn't with Yanni, knocking back gin and tonics like a good un and trying to make sympathetic eyes at the stewardesses, as if to say *I've nothing to do with this cretin.*

In New York the heat and humidity was fierce and as Sebastian wiped his brow, Yanni scoffed, "This is *tipota*, in Santorini we see this as mild spring day."

Sebastian, his lined suit creased beyond repair, felt a hatred for this bounder like he'd never felt in his whole shallow life and resolved, soon as this business was concluded, he was going to kill the fucker slowly and whisper as he died, "That's not heat, brother, it's just a mild slashing of your olive stinking throat."

Ah, the things to look forward to.

Then they were in a cab and heading for Queens. Who'd said anything about staying in Queens? Didn't the fellow have the decency to consult him about their travel arrangements? He was planning on getting a couple of rooms at the Mansfield, a small hotel he'd read about in a cheap mystery novel once; it sounded classy and was right across the road from The Algonquin. Couldn't ask for a better pedigree than that. But Yanni, lighting up a Karelia in the cab, didn't care about pedigree. So off to Queens they went.

Blowing smoke in Sebastian's face, Yanni said, "We stay with my family in Astoria, they help us track the she-devil. She has Greek blood, they will track her down."

Sebastian finally found his voice, said, "Actually, old chap, I'd rather stay in midtown and we can meet up later, let you reunite with your family in peace."

Yanni, his eyes as black as hell, squeezed Sebastian's thigh, hard—the animal had a grip like a vise—and said, "You don't make decisions. I tell you how it is, you say *epaharisto poli*. You get to leave when this is done, you understand, *mallakas?*"

He did.

The family were a nightmare and, lordy, how many of them were they, enough to storm Manhattan by themselves…and noisy, radios blaring, everybody roaring in Greek, tons of kissing and hugging, only not for Sebastian, whom they looked at with derision. No one said a word to him. It was like *My Big Fat Greek Wedding* without the one-liners.

At dinner, more talk in Greek. It sounded like six arguments were going on at once. Sebastian couldn't understand a thing, just wandered around, trying not to get in the way.

One of the uncles, he noticed, had his wallet sticking out of his back pocket, just begging to be snatched. Sebastian often wondered why people were careless with their valuables. Were they trying to give their money away? Out of sheer boredom, Sebastian snatched it, not expecting to find much. The guy's hair was a mess and he was wearing a horrendous shirt open to his belly button, proudly displaying a chunky wooden necklace—not exactly the look of a man of wealth.

When the fellow discovered his wallet was missing there was the usual fuss with everyone talking at once, helping him look around for it. During the commotion, Sebastian managed to slip out of the apartment without Yanni seeing. He sprinted around the corner and then two more blocks, hopped a turnstile. A subway was at the station, ready to depart, and Sebastian yelled, "Hold the doors!"

A homeless guy put his hand in front of one of the doors, delaying the close, and Sebastian managed to slip inside in the nick of time.

"Thank you, squire," he said. If he'd had some American coins he would've tipped the kind fellow, but he didn't. He settled for shaking the man's hand, a gesture neither of them enjoyed very much.

He rode the subway into Manhattan, proud of his ingenuity. He was a cunning ol' chappie, wasn't he?

It had been ages since he'd been to the city and he was planning to check into his usual room at the Mansfield—those kind fellows always gave him the top floor suite—and then take in some of the sights. He could do with some good food as well. There was a Brazilian restaurant in midtown he quite liked where the maitre d' was a good sport and always gave him the best table in the place and, oh yes, free drinks. He didn't know what they put in those bloody drinks but the last time he'd gone there he'd left so drunk he'd fallen over a pile of garbage on the curb and not gotten up for the better part of an hour.

At the Fifty-ninth Street stop, Sebastian disembarked and was about to climb the stairs when he heard, "Where you think you going, Brit boy?"

He thought he must be hallucinating but he turned around and sure enough Yanni was there. The bloody hell?

Covering his anguish with a sarcastic grin, Sebastian said, "I was just going for a bit of a stroll, care to join me?"

Back in captivity, or Queens, Sebastian spent days watching reruns of *The Odd Couple* and drinking that thick treacle they called coffee. The only thing that made it at all palatable was if you put a nip of Metaxa in it. And Heavens to Betsy, the Greeks might be a pain in the arse, no slur on their homoerotic heritage, but they sure did keep an awful lot of booze in the house.

Another saving grace: One of the women of the house, Irini, had that dark sultry look, the doe-brown eyes and one of those lush Greek figures that so quickly ran to fat but until then was simmering hot. Her English was almost American, with only a slight Greek inflection. She was forever cleaning and each time he got a buzz building, giggling away at Oscar and Felix, there she'd be, telling—not asking, mind, telling—him to move his big English legs out of the way. The drinks, the reruns, and Irina helped him keep his mind off his situation.

Which was looking worse each day. The men were pulling out all the stops to find Angela, but so far had found nothing, zilch, *tipota*. Like she'd vanished off the island of Manhattan, assuming she'd actually made it there in the first place. And Yanni's brood were seriously pissed. The Greek network was good and they prided themselves on tracking any Greek, anywhere, but it wasn't happening. And Sebastian was worried all that anger would wind up being let out in his direction someday soon.

Irini, hands on her hips, her wedding band shining, asked Sebastian, "Why you no help the men, you sit here all day, doing nothing?"

But he spotted a slight sheen of moisture above her lip and realized, this filly wanted rogering, a tad of the old Billy Bunter. And by golly, he was the chap to do it.

He said, "I could find her in five minutes."

Her eyes widened, and she asked, looking a bit like a mare in heat, "How?"

He gestured around the cramped living room, said, "They keep me a virtual prisoner, if I had access to a laptop, I'd have her tracked in no time."

She said, "I have a laptop. For my studies."

He wondered if there was a course in sweeping.

She lowered her eyes demurely, said, "It is in my bedroom."

He rose languidly. Sebastian tried never to do anything in a hurry unless it was…flee.

He said, "Show me what you've got."

Her room was filled with talismans—the evil eye, a mega statue of Makarios—and lo and fucking behold, in the middle of all this devotion, a poster of Guns N' Roses.

That was all she wrote. He rode her on the flokati rug and get this, the bitch bit him, twice, till he asked in his best Brit tone, "Try not to bite the merchandise."

Afterwards, still sweaty and naked, he opened the laptop and got Google to work its dark magic. His one idea was to find an address for Angela's ex, that Max Fisher bloke she'd complained about so much. Instead, he read about Fisher's bloody arrest. He was simply appalled to discover that Fisher had been a drug dealer. What sort of man had Angela been associating herself with? As if there had been any doubt, he was certain now he'd been the classiest lay she'd ever had.

But arrested, this wasn't good at all. He'd been hoping Fisher could help them find Angela. How could he help them from a jail cell in Attica?

But then he thought, who knows. That Hannibal Lecter chap had been able to help Jodie Foster from his jail cell in that movie, the *Lambs* one. Maybe this Fisher could be of at least *some* use.

When you've only got one straw, you grasp at it.

One article from the *New York Post* gave the address where Fisher was serving his sentence; that not only meant Sebastian knew where to find him, it also meant Angela knew. He'd have laid stiff odds that she had paid him at least one visit there, and who knows, maybe she'd come more than once. Maybe he'd know where she was and could steer them to her.

Sebastian was downright proud of his ingenuity. A bloody Sherlock Holmes, he was. It would have taken the Greeks, what, five years to come up with this angle?

Irini gave him a cold Amstel and, by golly, it was good. She said, "You must be quick."

He winked at her, said, "You sang a different tune on the rug."

She said, "If Marko comes home, he will cut your balls off."

He got right on it.

Sixteen

*"The man who shoots people in the legs for effect,
thinks that I might have been unnecessarily violent?"*
ALLAN GUTHRIE, *Two-Way Split*

First thing Sino was gonna do when he got out—come
at that *bandajo* Max Fisher hard. His two weeks in the
hole, he been thinking about that shit all the time,
thinking of different ways to make the man feel pain.

Fuckin' Fisher. Sino shoulda taken his *gorda* ass out
himself, made a mistake out saucering that shit to that
puta Carlito. You can't trust a Mexican to do nothing
'cept make burritos and even then, check out all the
PR's they hire at Taco Bell.

Fourteen *dias* in the hole and it didn't break Sino at
all. Made him stronger, more *duro*. He spent the time
workin' out down there, doin' a thousand push-ups a
day, and thinkin' maybe he do Fisher with his hands.
Take his time with it, maybe start in on his face, to
hear some bones breakin', that was always a lot of fun.
Fisher, the *bandajo*, would be screamin' and beggin',
and that'd only get Sino goin' more. Maybe he'd break
his arms, then his legs, all the bones in his body one by
one, till he was one big pile of *maricon* bones. But he'd

still be alive 'cause, yeah, that's what Sino wanted, to make the man stay alive, to keep feeling pain.

Or, maybe he should burn Fisher's ass? Yeah, seeing a man die in *fuera* was like a fuckin' fiesta.

Wait, hold up, Sino had a better way to do it. He'd get a shank and cut him up real good. Name's Fisher, right? So Sino gonna cut him up like a fish. Do it nice and slow too. Little cuts first, make the man see some blood, then get in deeper, make him see some *real* blood. He'd cut his whole body up but save the best part for last. Man say he cut a man's dick off, like to talk about it all the time? Maybe Sino gonna cut off Fisher's dick, feed it to him, *then* kill him.

Make that *bandajo* wish he never took that pie from Sino.

Angela had the cash, now all she had to do was trade it for the weapons and the car Max wanted. Way back, her boyfriend Dillon, that wannabe boyo—and what a piece of work he'd been—had introduced her to Sean, a genuine boyo, as lethal as they came. She'd seen him roll a dead cop in a blanket and dump him like an old carpet. Sean was from that fierce and ferocious school of old paramilitaries, the sort that'd never surrender, they'd sooner go down in a blaze of armalites and were always tooled to the max.

Sean, whose only claim to an income came from irregular shifts as a taxi driver, had a stammer and an atrocious record with women. He'd get seriously drunk, approach the most attractive woman in a room, and with his stammer go, "I'm Se…a…n…I've…n-n-n-n-n-o…job……will you let me r-r-r-r-r-ride you?"

Subtle, right? It was certainly clear and direct communication, but he was batting zero.

Angela knew he had the hots for her, due to the drool that leaked from his lips any time he looked at her. Time to make it sing.

He lived in an abandoned warehouse on the Lower East Side. He didn't bother too much with security. His rep was well known—you rip off the boyos, dig a deep hole.

Angela knew how to visit a murderous mick: Bring a seven course feast—six bottles of the black and a litre of Jameson.

She climbed the shabby, worn stairs to his apartment on the second floor, seeing rats scurrying in the stairwell corners. They didn't trouble her. After Greece, four-legged rodents were the least of her fears.

She knocked on his door, which had a massive Green Harp on it. He pulled it open and she thought, *Jesus, he's gone downhill*.

Never an oil painting, he was dressed in a Galway Hurling T-shirt and baggy combats. He was barefoot and his face, under the red beard…it looked like someone had taken a blowtorch to it. Probably someone had —though Sean was still here, so whoever did it was surely now feeding whatever still swam in the East River. She noticed the SIG in his left hand, held casually.

Took him a moment to register who she was, then he went, "A…n…g-g-g-g-g-g-gela?"

Nothing wrong with his memory.

She smiled, said, *"Conas ata tu?" How are you?*

You want to lure a boyo, talk Irish.

He smiled. Most of his front teeth missing, and his gums, burned because he'd forgotten to close his mouth when they used the blowtorch. She did the real smart thing, the sort of move that kept her, if only precariously, in the game. She hugged him tight. He was an Irish man, and with that bust up against him, he was already signed, sealed and fooked.

Then Angela said, "I'll be needing some weapons and a car," and Sean went, "I d-d-d-dri-v-ve a c-c-c-c-c-c-c-c-cab."

She oh so accidently brushed his cock. The bastard was rock hard. She wondered how long it had been since he'd gotten laid. Yeah, how long since the Pope gave a shite?

She said, "Let's have a jar. You still drink, Sean, darling?"

Let sensuality leak all over his name. He'd come before the next teardrop fell.

He said, "I...I...t-t-t-t-t-ta...k-k-k-ke......the od-d-d-d-d-d jar, right......e...n-n-n-nough."

She went into his tiny kitchen and surprise, it was spotless. Bachelors, they went one of two ways, became total slobs—i.e., Max—or became obsessive-compulsive. He was the latter.

She found some Galway Crystal Glasses, those babies went for a fortune, weighed serious tonnage

and were no doubt an heirloom from his beloved
mother. The micks loved their Mums; no doubt there
was some fookin' Irish lace tablecloth neatly folded
and lovingly stored somewhere in the place. She made
the working stiff's version of *The Black and Tan*, always
amused the boyos, and they were one hard fooking act
to amuse. Ask the Brits.

A large shot of the Jay and add just the right amount
of Guinness, it was an acquired taste but it got you
there, fast.

She brought the glasses in and, indicating the im-
maculate sofa, cooed, "Join me *a gra.*"

Nervously, he did, his combats showing a massive
tent. She handed him the glass, said, *"Slainte amach."*

The very personal version of cheers.

His hand shook as he took it and they clinked the
precious glasses and drank deep. Well, Sean drained
his, and she hopped up, said, "Let me freshen that,
amach, and we'll talk guns and why you're going to
help me."

She added three fingers of the Jay and not so much
of the black.

He half finished that, a dribble coming from his lips,
tried, "A-a-a-a-ngela......I......d-d-d-d-dr...iv-v-v-ve...
...a......cab."

She put her hand on his dick, said, "I always had a
thing for you, Sean."

The continued use of his name and with such ten-
derness, plus the booze, was really screwing with his

head. Not that it looked like it took much, since the blowtorch incident; looked like his mind was mostly scrambled eggs anyway.

She unzipped him, asked, "Would you like me to take care of that stallion you have rearing up there?"

Would he fooking ever. He'd have sold the mother's linen, glasses and grave for it.

She said, "I'm going to be your woman, okay, darling?"

He nodded, too weak to speak, and she asked, "The guns?"

He stuttered, "How......m-m-m-m-m-man...y...... d-d-d-d-o......y-y-y-y-you, you...y-y-you......w-w-w-w-w-want?"

Seventeen

"He had to hit him, but only him and only once.
After that it was sadism."
JIM FUSILLI, *Closing Time*

In the morning before the night when all hell broke loose, Max met Paula for an interview session for the book. She'd arranged to have another private meeting, wearing something super low-cut, but this time the view didn't give Max any liftoff.

"Sorry, babe, the wedding's cancelled, kaput, finito."

Said it stone-faced, no emotion, figured, Why sugarcoat it? Gotta hit hard, hit low, and hit early. And, man, he loved delivering bad news—what a fuckin' rush! It reminded him of the days when he was a CEO and he got to fire people. That was the best part of his job—crushing the assholes' dreams, watching them fucking melt.

"Oh," she asked, "and why's that?"

He could tell she wasn't taking it well. She'd probably been planning for the big day, telling all her friends. Fuck, she'd probably had the band picked out.

"No offense, baby, but something bigger and better came along. A lot bigger and a lot better."

Still hurting she asked, "This won't affect the book, will it?"

"No, my motto is, Always do what you say you're gonna do."

"All right, then," she said.

Was she stifling tears? Yeah, probably.

But she was a pro and managed to put it behind her. She started in with her questions:

> *Do you remember your first meeting with Angela Petrakos?*

> *Was it love at first sight?*

> *What are your impressions of her boyfriend at the time, Thomas Dillon, AKA Popeye?*

It was rough for Max, having to relive that dark period in his life. Well, it wasn't really, but he acted like it was, knowing that sounding like it had been painful and traumatic was what sold books. Wasn't that how Oprah did it?

Then Paula started asking the harder questions like: Did you want to kill your wife? Did you plot with Angela and Dillon to kill your wife? And—the most potentially incriminating of all—did you hire Dillon to kill your wife?

If Max hadn't been flying so high, if he hadn't been in the midst of the power trip to end all power trips, he might've thought it over first and realized that confessing to his wife's murder, and admitting involvement in other murders and crimes he'd never been charged for, wasn't exactly in his best interest. But, hell, he let it fly. It was the equivalent of an outright confession, details that could get him the death penalty.

But right then Max wasn't thinking penalty, he was thinking publicity, he was thinking celebrity. That was what it was all about, right? Why hold back on the meat? You're gonna open the door, open it all the way.

And Paula, yeah, she was eating it up, telling him how excited she was about the project, and how the biggest challenge would be to fit all this amazing material into one book.

"I might have to make it into a trilogy," she said, and Max suddenly had a vision of the great Hollywood trilogies. *Star Wars*, *The Godfather*, *Shrek*, *Revenge of the Nerds*.

Imagining billions of dollars in DVD sales, merchandising, box office receipts, imagining walking onstage to accept his Oscar, Max made another impulsive decision.

He said, "You wanna get a first-hand look at The M.A.X. in action? What're you doing tonight at, say, midnight?"

"I don't have plans," Paula said. "Why?"

"How'd you like to ride in a getaway car with The M.A.X. and the rest of his crew?"

Yep, he told her all about the whole prison break, down to the last detail. Probably not a good idea to share this info with a woman he hardly knew—and, worse, a woman he'd just fucking *dumped*—but the escape was going to climax the greatest moment in his life, and he wanted his biographer there to witness it.

Later, heading back to his cell, Max was still pumped, thinking how lucky a thing it was to be Max Fisher, when he saw Sino. He'd probably just been released from the hole—he was in cuffs, being walked along by a guard. When Sino saw Max he stopped and the guard stopped with him. Sino gave Max the dead-eye glare, and his nostrils flared and his jaw shifted as he grinded his teeth. Max didn't back down. He shot back with his own mean-ass look, feeling like he was in a Western, two *hombres* staring each other down before the big shootout.

Then, suddenly, Max smiled widely. He made his thumb and forefinger into the shape of a gun, pointed it at Sino, and bent his thumb, pulling the trigger.

Man, the look on the big lump of meat's face was fucking priceless.

Paula went back to the motel, real disappointed. She wouldn't be the next Mrs. Max Fisher—how would she ever get over it? She laughed, thinking, *Was the guy for real or what*? Sometimes she thought he was fucking with her, with all the weird accents, the tough talk, the outrageous stories. It had to be some kind of schtick, a put-on. She was always waiting for him to crack up and say, Got you good there, huh? But it had never happened. And now he claimed he was staging a prison break? Probably a delusion like the rest of it. But hey, if it happened, she was going to be there to chronicle it. A first-person account of her subject escaping from Attica? It would like Junger getting a chance to ride the boat into the perfect storm.

After she parked her car, she walked to the soda machine near the motel's office and bought a Tab—had to watch the figure if she was going to attract maximum babe-age. She figured she'd find some girl-girl porn on TV, rub one out, then try to find some decent food for lunch, not an easy task in this shithole town. After the incident at the bar, she was trying to keep a low profile. For all she knew it was legal to shoot dykes up here. Jesus, up here you wouldn't even know you were in New York. It was like a fucking red state.

As she headed back toward her room she stopped and did a double-take when she saw Lee Child walking toward her with another guy. What the hell was Lee Child doing up here? Was he on an author tour? Was the guy his media escort? Was there a mystery bookstore in Attica? Were there any bookstores in Attica? Were there any *books* in Attica? Hard to imagine that they even knew how to read up here.

Back in her straight days she'd had a big thing for Lee—who didn't, right?—and now she was so flustered, so starstruck, she couldn't even say hello or call out his name. She just watched with a dumb expression as he and the guy he was with went into their room.

She wondered: Why was he staying at this crummy motel? Wasn't he loaded?

Then she had a thought that terrified her—was he up here to try to steal the story out from under her? She knew he was doing well these days, at the top of the *Times* list and all, but every writer was always on the lookout for the next big thing. Hell, Paula herself had gotten most of her ideas for books at the bar at one mystery convention or another. Piss-drunk authors would tell her their best ideas, then forget the conversations in the morning. Maybe Lee saw The M.A.X as his next blockbuster, his big move into true crime. The more she thought about it, the more sense it made.

She marched over to room 16, started banging on the door.

If Sebastian thought riding in an airplane with Yanni had been a dreadful experience, and spending time with his family in Astoria had been painful, then riding in a car with him was a full-blown nightmare. Had the fellow heard that there'd been an invention—a true breakthrough—called deodorant? Lordy, the smell of the man! And he didn't even have the decency to open the passenger-side window. He had all the controls on his side of the car, and he insisted on riding with the windows closed and no air conditioning. He mentioned something about allergies or whatnot, but Sebastian knew it was only to inflict maximum torture on him.

They passed a rest area and Sebastian had never

been so excited to see a McDonald's in his entire life. Naturally the mad Greek wouldn't let them stop, though. He said something about "making good time" and "saving gas," but Sebastian figured he was just being an ass.

They'd left at the crack of dawn and arrived in Attica at around noon. Oh, lucky them! Talk about a party town! Sebastian honestly didn't know how his life had descended to this horrid state. A few weeks ago he'd been living it up on Santorini and now he was in a place that made those Western ghost towns you saw in the movies seem lively, being dragged around by the Greek from hell.

Their room wasn't ready. That's correct—room, singular. Yanni insisted on sharing a room, even sharing a king-size bed, so Sebastian couldn't slip away.

"Oh, come on now, you can trust me," Sebastian said as they stood at the front desk. The sarcasm couldn't have been thicker.

"We sleep in same bed," Yanni insisted, "and you wear handcuffs."

The clerk heard this and with a concerned look said, "Uh, sir, this is a family motel."

"*Please*," Sebastian said. "I'll treat myself to a nice-looking chappie every once in a while like any good un, but I'd rather die than be a bottom for this cretin."

"*Cretan?*" Yanni said, deeply insulted. "Yanni is not from Crete, my family live on Santorini nine hundred years." Sebastian apologized for misremembering.

They waited in—where else?—the car until the room had been serviced. As soon as they got in, there was a hammering at the door. Sebastian answered it, saw a woman there, full figured, longish brown hair—attractive enough, but something about her made him think, *lesbian*.

She was saying, "Son of a bitch. You think you can steal The M.A.X. from me, you fucking British bastard."

Sebastian replied with an ultra polite, "Sorry, have we met?"

"Yeah, at last year's ThrillerFest. I told you how much I loved Jack Fucking Reacher, remember?"

Going along he said, "Oh, of course, silly me. How could I forget?" He had, of course, no idea who she was, but he said, "I'd invite you in, my sweet, but alas, I'm otherwise occupied."

Then Yanni was behind him, naturally, never more than Karelia spit away, and he asked angrily, "Who is this cunt?"

Sebastian said, "I say, old chap, steady on."

The woman looked at the Greek and said, "What did you call me?"

Sebastian, if not always ready, was most definitely nearly always prepared, had taken some hooch from the Greek's home, and said, "Now let's all calm down. Come in, gell, have a drink, and dammit, we'll thrash this out between us like civilized human beings."

"Where you get booze in this shithole?" Yanni asked, and the woman asked, "The fuck is a *gell*?"

But they took it inside, neither of them the sort to turn down a drink.

Sebastian got the two plastic toothbrushing cups from the bathroom and produced a battered tin cup he still carried from his Chatwin days, he really believed he'd lived like ol' Bruce. Then, with a flourish, out of the Gladstone bag came a bottle of scotch. Sebastian murmured, "Alas, we're all out of ice, the maid has the day off."

He poured lethal measures and nobody complained. He toasted, "To jolly good company, what?"

No one answered him.

They drank in silence, getting the good stuff to ignite in their system. When they'd killed the scotch and the contents of the room's minibar, the woman said, "You're not fucking Lee Child."

Sebastian nearly laughed at the double entendre.

"Child?" Yanni asked. "Where child?"

Then Sebastian, scotch calm, said, "Ah, you've rumbled me, the game is up as old Sherlock used to say, or was that afoot? I'm actually Lee's half brother. We don't get on, and truly, I'm chuffed with his success."

Yanni, tired of a conversation he was having trouble following, pointed his finger at the woman, asked, "Why are you here?"

She'd drunk the scotch way too fast and it loosened her tongue.

"I thought he was stealing my book," she said, wagging a finger in Sebastian's direction.

"Your book? What are you talking about?" Sebastian asked.

She told them all about some bloody awful book she was writing about Max Fisher and Angela, and about the murders Fisher had committed, and how he'd apparently become a feared man in prison. Sounded like a real winner all right. The punters would surely be rushing to the stores to buy that one.

Then she told them about a prison break at midnight.

Sebastian had a lightbulb moment, said, "Prison break?"

"Yeah, there're going to be riots, big riots. I'm a big riot!" She looked at her glass. "What's in this shit anyway?"

Sebastian egged her on, going, "So about the prison break…"

"Oh, yeah, it's at midnight tonight, at least that's what The M.A.X. said. The M.A.X.!" She laughed. "You believe that's what he calls himself now? He put a 'the' in front of his name and he has initials. Initials! Is he a character or what? I'm gonna make a fortune on this book and Pulitzer, look out. Oh, and Angela, I'm dying to meet that crazy bitch. She's going to be in the getaway car with some IRA guy. Is this gonna be a trip or what?"

Yanni put a switchblade to the woman's throat said, "Shut up, cunt, and take us to this she-devil who killed my cousin. *Now.*"

The woman continued to smile drunkenly until her eyes focused on the knife and she started to scream. Yanni backhanded her in the face and knocked her to the floor.

Sebastian upended his tin cup and, patting its bottom, drained the last trickle of scotch. "Oh, lordy," he said, "was that really necessary?"

Eighteen

Let the riots begin…

Max was dozing when the riot began. He was gently stirred by Rufus who said, "It's on, boss."

Max, still groggy, heard what sounded like the seventh circle of hell and smelled smoke, lots of smoke. He asked, "The riot?"

A click sounded and their cell door slid open.

Rufus said, "They already got in the control room, yo. The man, he gonna come down hard, we got to move, know what I'm sayin', make it to the laundry truck. Once they bring in the troops, we gonna be fried meat."

He handed Max a bandana, said, "Rap the rag round your mouth, breathe through your nose, and stay real close, yo. Gonna be biblical out there."

Max was terrified and exhilarated all at once, and the bandana, shit, he felt like The Boss. He grabbed the bottle of Chivas, swallowed a fiery amount and handed it to Rufus who drained the rest. Then Max picked up a broomstick they'd stowed under the bottom bunk, broke it in half, said, "Rock 'n' roll."

The tier was chaotic, cons running everywhere, and Max saw one of the guards being held by a Crip, broken bottle to his neck. The Crip looked at Max, winked, then slashed the guard's throat.

Max felt the Chivas rebel and he let Rufus get ahead as he bent over, gagging. Then, out of the smoke, came Sino, his face streaked with blood like war paint, like a deranged angel of death. He hissed, "Hey, *bandajo*, where you goin'? I'm gonna cut yo' ass in a hundred pieces and then I'm gonna burn yo' *puta* ass, bitch."

Max was unable to move and as Sino closed in on him he thought, *After everything, this is it.* He felt his bowels loosen and then Sino's eyes went wide, his mouth made a silent *O* and he looked down at the shaft of wood that had been driven through his chest. He fell forward.

Arma, leader of the white supremacists, bent down, put his boot on Sino's back, pulled out the shaft, said, "I'll be needing that, spic."

Max was trying to form words that would express his thanks when a crew of Crips appeared, armed with homemade clubs, knives, even a frying pan.

Arma turned to face them, then said to Max, "We'll go down like white men, right, boy?"

Max thought, *Like fuck we will*, and took off, looking back to see Arma disappear beneath a sea of Crips.

Then Rufus grabbed Max's arm, pulled him through the inferno.

Before Rufus could drag Max to the next tier, a guard came running. It was the guy, Malis, who'd once been nice to Max in the yard. He stopped, begged, "Save me."

A tiny con grabbed the guard and said, "Your face is dirty," and threw a jarful of acid at him. Max watched in disbelief as Malis' face began to literally melt, peel off in layers. The con dropped the empty jar and ran, a knife coming loose from his belt and clattering to the floor as he went. Max whipped it up almost by reflex, grateful to have something deadly he could hold in his hand rather than just a broken broomstick.

Rufus was pulling Max along again, going, "Gotta get yo' ass in gear now, boss."

As Rufus dragged Max through the smoke and chaos, it hit Max hard that he hadn't killed anybody yet. What the fuck? He was The M.A.X., the alpha dog, the Big Boss, the Springsteen of the Big House, and he was what, getting yanked along like he was some kind of fucking sissy? He had to take somebody out, that's what he had to do. His rep was on the line. He had to show Rufus that The M.A.X. was one sick-ass mutha-fucka. Also, he knew that this was a moment he'd look back on his entire life. This moment would define him, make him proud. Didn't all the World War II vets go on and on about all the nips they took out? Didn't the Vietnam dudes reminisce about the gooks they'd blown away? This was Max's war, the high point of his life, and if he choked now, didn't come through with at least one killing, he'd never forgive himself.

They went down a flight of stairs, stepping over

bodies, then headed toward the delivery entrance. Up ahead in the smoke Max spotted a guy. He had a flashback to the time he'd killed all those drug dealers, blew 'em to smithereens, and that gave him the confidence boost he needed.

Holding the knife, he broke free from Rufus and charged the guy. He was roaring as he ran, making crazed animal noises like Mel Gibson in *Braveheart*. He plunged the blade into the guy's back, and it was fucking harder than it looked in the movies. It wouldn't go in more than an inch at first and he had to use both his hands to work the blade in there. The whole time he was screaming his ass off, drooling like a rabid dog.

When he was through he let go of the body, letting it fall to the floor. The guy looked dead all right. Fucking wasted.

He wiped the blade of the knife on the dead man's pants, then looked back at Rufus, expecting to see a terrified, respectful look from his soldier.

Instead he got, "Fuck you do that for, boss?"

Max, still pumped, said, "Didn't like the way fuckin' Crip was lookin' at me. Bro had to go."

Rufus said, "Man, that wasn't no motherfuckin' Crip. That was our ride, yo."

Max didn't know what the fuck he was talking about, said, "The fuck're you talkin' about?"

"That was K, man. He was with us an' shit. He was gonna ride our asses out in the truck."

Max felt like, well, like a fucking moron, but he had

to cover and went, "Your *man* was planning to double-cross us. Soon as we cleared the gates he would've wasted us both."

Rufus wasn't buying it, went, "K wasn't gonna double-cross nobody, yo. K was my boy an' shit. Man, I been with the nigga since I got inside, knew the bitch on the outside, too. I been plannin' this breakout with him, shit, since my first day in lockup."

It was starting to hit Max just how badly he'd fucked up.

He said, "I know you don't wanna believe your own man would fuck you over, but I got spies working for me, okay? And this guy, J—"

"K," Rufus said.

"K, L, M, N, O, P," Max said. "Who gives a shit what his name was? The guy was a fuckin' rat, all right? So forget about him. He's better off dead."

Max reached into K's pocket, found a set of keys, then Rufus said, "Yo, K got the uniforms too. Gotta put that shit on."

Max found the uniforms, tucked under K's shirt. They were bloody, but what the hell were you gonna do?

They put the uniforms on as fast as they could, then they made it all the way down and the laundry truck was right there. Shit, this stupid plan might work.

They were about to get in when Max heard, "Hey, dude."

He turned and saw Arma, battered, covered in

blood. Shit, he looked like Bruce Willis at the end of the first *Die Hard*. He was still holding the bloody wooden shaft, going, "You ain't turnin' nigger on me, are you, dude?"

Angela and Sean were in the sedan at the meeting point, about a mile away from the prison. They could hear the alarms sounding and knew the riot was on. Angela had taken time over her appearance, thinking, What does a girl wear to a riot besides a fookin' Kevlar vest? She'd decided on basic black. Not only was it appropriate but it made you look thin, she hoped. Sean, well fashion was not his gig. He was wearing the green army jacket beloved of the boyos, they practically slept in them, along with his *de rigeur* combat pants and Doc Martens with steel toe cap. On his knee, he had a pump shotgun, and there was a mess of other weapons in the back. Angela had selected the SIG, she was familiar with that baby and you know, it sort of accessorized her outfit. Sean reached in his jacket, took out a flask, drank deep, offered it to her, and she took it, swallowed, raw Jay and by Jaysus, it burned.

Sean said, "A…a…a……d-d-d-d-d-drop……of…of the…c-c-c-c-creature."

He reached in his other pocket. If he produced snacks, she'd shoot him.

He didn't, but he did take out a grenade.

Catching her eye, he said, "Been sav-v-v-ing it f-f-f-f-f-for…a…s-s-s-spec…ial…occ-c-c-c-c-c-asion."

Even from where they were, they could see the

smoke rising from the prison and the wail of sirens
had started, like a hurt banshee. The copters would be
there soon. She looked down to check out the SIG in
her lap and saw a tent in Sean's pants. She muttered,
"Like, *now?*"

Not far from them but out of their line of vision were
Sebastian and Yanni. They were watching Angela's car.

Yanni was slugging from a goatskin bag—where the
hell had he got that?—and Sebastian knew it was ouzo.
Sebastian was taking the traditional route, gin and
tonic, in a plastic bottle. It was whispering to him,
"Nothing to worry about."

Right.

In the distance, Attica was burning, but here things
were calm. For now anyway. Sebastian had begged
Yanni not to just rush over to Angela's car and blast
away, and for once Yanni had listened to him. It was
the possibility there might be money to be had if they
waited for Fisher to show up that had convinced him.
They were here to wreak vengeance—but a little profit
would be nice, too.

Yanni had a Ruger and the metal glinted as he
turned it this way and that, waiting. He handled it like
someone who had long experience with weapons.
Sebastian was carrying a Walther PPK, for the love of
Bond and Britain. He'd once gone pheasant hunting
and managed to hit the gamekeeper, to the delight and
hoots of his fellow drunken shooters. He'd give a lot to
be back there now.

Paula was lying across the back seat, still sleeping off her booze and the clout to the head.

Yanni shifted suddenly and they saw a laundry truck pull up. An old guy—Fisher—and a huge black man jumped out. They piled into Angela's car and the car pulled slowly away, no massive getaway, just a cautious stealing pace.

Yanni hit the ignition and smiled grimly, said, *"Poli mallakas."*

Sebastian took a long swig from the gin and hoped he wouldn't bloody castrate himself during the ride.

Max knew he needed to think of something quick, went with, "I was just here gettin' set to kill this here nigger."

Rufus, the fucking idiot, said, "You was doin' *what*, boss?"

Still calling him boss, just what Arma needed to hear.

But it didn't matter because Arma wasn't buying the crap anyway. He said, "What y'all wearin' laundry clothes for? Y'all tryin' to run out and leave your Aryan brothers to burn? I save yer sorry ass back there and you turn coyote and leave me?"

Max's mouth sagged open, but he couldn't think of anything to say. He couldn't figure out how Arma had survived the heap of Crips who'd descended on him.

"I shoulda known," Arma said. "Shackin' up with the dirtiest nigger in this here prison. He probably put so much a his black meat in you all them nights, he been gettin' to you, made you black yerself. Ain't that

right, Fisher? You don't know what color you are no
more, do you?"

The sirens were blaring. Lockdown was going to
happen any second. If they were going to do this, they
had to do it now.

"I told you," Max said, "I'm gonna kill the guy, but I
want to do it in private. I just want it to be me and him,
hombre a hombre."

Arma said, "I'll show you how it's done," and the
next second he was attacking Rufus, trying to stick his
shaft into the big man's neck. Rufus was fighting back,
but Arma was quicker and the wood gave him a longer
reach.

Knowing this would be another defining moment in
his life, Max went over and drove the knife into Arma's
back. This time he knew how do it, getting it in the
first time, through all the bone and muscle and stuff.

"Fisher, you fuckin' nigger," Arma said.

He tried to turn, bring his shaft up to use on Max,
but he crumpled to the ground.

Holy shit, killing people was fun! Max felt like a
hunter, like a real fucking man.

Max left the knife in Arma's back and said to Rufus,
"You okay?"

Rufus said, "Yeah, just some blood, ain't no nothin'.
But, yo, boss, you got some moves, yo."

They got in the truck and headed out of the prison.
There was so much chaos at the gate, the guard took a
cursory look at Max and Rufus and waved them
through.

"We did it, boss," Rufus said. "We really fuckin' did it."

Max was still lost in his own world, high from killing Arma. No wonder crackheads killed people, it was fucking addicting. Max couldn't wait to kill again. He wanted more. More, more, more.

Rufus gave Max directions and he followed them. About a mile away from the prison on a dirt road they approached a dark sedan. Max drove the laundry truck off the side of the road, out of view, and then he and Rufus ditched the truck and jogged over to the sedan.

Angela and her IRA friend were in the front. Max and Rufus got in the back and Max said, "Where the fuck is Paula?"

"Who?" Angela asked.

"The big-chested girl? My biographer," Max said, like it was obvious.

"The fook're you talking about?" Angela asked.

He didn't have time to explain, or to wait.

"Drive," he said, and the IRA guy drove away.

Max leaned over the seat, gave Angela a big fat one on her full lips. Man, she smelled good, like fucking Irish Spring. He remembered how much he loved fucking Irish chicks and he couldn't wait to give Angela the meat tonight. He said, "Man, I can't wait to give you the meat tonight, bitch."

"Who're you callin' bitch, you fookin' cunt."

Ah, the mouth on her. He loved it.

Rufus was still babbling, "We did it, boss, we did it, yo. We really done an' did it."

Then Max looked back and noticed the car behind them. It wasn't directly behind them—it might've been thirty or forty yards back—but it was still unsettling to see it there, tagging along.

"I think that car's following us," Max said.

Angela looked back and said, "What car?"

"There's one car on the fucking road," Max said. "Pick one."

Angela was built, but he'd forgotten how dumb she was.

Then the IRA guy spoke his first words. Well, if you call it speaking.

"I'm p-p-p-p-p-positive…the c-c-c-car isn't…f-f-f-f-f-f-fah-fah-fah-fah…"

"The fuck is he saying?" Max asked.

"I haven't a clue," Angela said.

"He saying ain't nobody back there, yo," Rufus said.

Figured, two idiots could understand each other.

Max looked back again, but the headlights were gone.

"Just sit back and start celebratin', boss," Rufus said. "We did it. We really motherfuckin' did it."

Nineteen

"I wanted more. Give me more."
MEGAN ABBOTT, *Queenpin*

Angela needed a shower, a drink, to get laid and to get—of course, as always—rich.

The drive to the Canadian border had been bizarre. Sean, muttering stuff in his stammer that nobody could follow and Max insisting they were being followed. She'd forgotten how paranoid he'd always been, long before anyone got hurt. And she was still seething about him "putting the meat to her."

He would, like fook.

Angela was plain dumbfounded by the huge black man. With one hand he could have strangled them all and instead, he was brown-nosing Max, gazing at him with, there was no other word for it, total admiration. Was it some kind of gay thing? Prison does weird shite to people.

They reached the border just before dusk and Sean pulled into a trailer park, said as he checked his notes and found a key, "W-w-w-we're……nu-nu-num-b-b-b-b-ber…t-t-t-t-twenty s-s-s-six."

Nobody was saying much as they trudged their way to the trailer.

Angela couldn't believe it, she had finally hit bottom: trailer trash. She'd be here for life, wearing denim shorts, her hair permanently in rollers, no AC, and three snot-nosed brats wailing at her for sodas. And she'd have no man, of course.

She shuddered.

In the car, Max had reached over, asked, "Cold? Wait till I get in you, you'll be so hot."

She'd nearly gut shot the bollix then and there.

Someone had made slight preparations for their arrival. There was coffee, a thermos, three bunk beds and, sitting in the middle of the trailer, a bottle of Jay and about twenty beers.

No food.

Angela heard Max whine, "No food?"

Then he grabbed the bottle of Jay, said, no, *ordered*, "Y'all grab some glass or other, The M.A.X. has a toast to make."

Jameson out of Styrofoam is a travesty but Angela figured it was one of the least of the sins on her conscience.

Max said, "I toast our valiant rescuers, Angela and…" He paused, getting ready for his renowned wit, continued, "Sh-sh-sh-sh-sh-sh-sh…Sean."

No laughter, and the Irish guy was giving him a look that said, "You're dead."

Angela could see Max was confused by how badly his humor had backfired.

He added lamely, "The joint hasn't been built that could hold The M.A.X."

Later, Rufus was making hungry noises and Max was famished too. Since Sean had already passed out drunk, it was decided Rufus and Angela would head for the nearest grocery store—a 7-Eleven off the highway—and stock up. Rufus would drive, stay out of view, and Angela would do the shopping.

At first, Angela was a little, well, concerned about being alone with Rufus. After all, he was a big, scary-looking guy and he'd been locked up so long, he probably couldn't wait to get his big mitts all over a woman. But after what she'd been through in Greece, Angela wasn't about to let a man get the best of her, no matter how menacing he was. She had a gun with her, in her handbag, and God knows she wasn't afraid to use it.

In the car, Rufus was going on, telling her how great it was to be in the "outside" again and how the first thing he wanted to do was go see his mama in Syracuse. Angela was starting to zone out when she heard the word money.

Rabbit ears up, she echoed, "Money?"

"Yeah," Rufus said, "from the job I pulled 'fore they sent my ass to Attica. Me an' my crew we robbed a bank and shit. Got two hundred somethin' thousand dollars, but they never found it 'cause I buried it in my mama's backyard, that's why. So when I get home, first thing I'm gonna do after I kiss my mama hello and eat some a her fine apple pie is I'm gonna dig up that money, then I'm gonna go off, live in Mexico."

Suddenly Angela saw Rufus in a new light. He was no longer a scary, dangerous escaped convict who might rape and kill her. Now he was the sweet mama's boy with two hundred grand in his backyard who was going to be her ticket to her new life. And, besides, she'd always liked black guys. Okay, not more than any other type, but not less either, and he was a big strong guy, he could protect her; and despite whatever awful things he might have done to wind up in prison, compared to some of the other men she'd dated he was practically a saint.

She wanted to make sure he knew she was available and interested. So she said, "Just so you know, I'm just here, helping Max out, for old time's sake. We're not together or anything like that."

She could tell Rufus wanted her badly. Jaysus, it looked like his dick was about to burst though his pants.

He said, "Yo, that's good, cause I like you and shit, yo. I think you fine. I never seen a set a titties on a white woman before like the ones you got. You got big ol' black titties, know what I'm sayin'? They kinda like my gran'mas. Yo, I don't mean I been lookin' at my gran'ma's titties an' shit, but you know what I'm sayin'."

Angela knew there had to be a compliment in there somewhere and said, "Thank you, I'm so flattered."

Rufus continued, "But the way it is, yo', I don' wanna move in on the boss's action, know what I'm sayin'? I know how much the boss love your titties too. 'Fore we broke out, every night he was goin' on 'bout your titties, goin', Wait till you see my bitch's titties. I ain't callin' you bitch, that what The M.A.X. be callin' you.

He be goin', You're gonna love my bitch's titties, they so big, they're the best titties you ever seen. An' wanna know somethin'? Muthafucka was right."

Angela, thinking about that money, how it could change her fucking life, said, "Don't worry about Max. If you want my titties they're all yours."

They pulled into the lot next to the 7-Eleven.

Rufus cut the engine, said, "Mind if I kiss you? Been a long time since I kissed a woman. Talkin' about a natural-born woman, know what I'm sayin'?"

Angela batted her eyelashes, went, "I thought you'd never ask."

Wow, Rufus knew how to kiss! He was tender and slow and he really knew how to use that big, long tongue of his. Was Angela imagining it or was she feeling a serious spark between them? She couldn't remember the last time she'd enjoyed something as simple as a kiss with man.

There was no doubt what she had to do: Ditch Max and go with Rufus. Max was broke anyway, so what use was he? And she had a feeling this Rufus thing had legs, it was the real deal.

Rufus waited in the car. Before Angela left he said, "I'll be missin' yo ass, baby." He was such a sweet man, so thoughtful.

Angela stocked up on all the food Max had instructed her to buy: Yodels, Ring Dings, Fritos, Pop Tarts, lots of Slim Jims, etc. As she was paying at the register, she noticed a dark blue car pull up in the parking lot out front and just idle there. She didn't think much of it, though, just collected her change from the guy at the counter and wished him a good night.

She was imagining life in Mexico, as Mrs. Rufus, when she stepped outside and noticed the guy walking toward her through the shadowy lot. She couldn't see his face well but, fuck, there was no doubt he was Greek, and he looked familiar somehow. Then he passed under a lamppost and she saw why he looked familiar. He was a dead ringer for Georgios. She remembered the woman back in Santorini, vowing vengeance for Georgios' murder, and she knew this had to be connected. A voice inside her head was saying, Oh, come on, stop with the paranoia, you're starting to sound like Max. The Greek network for tracking people down is good, but it couldn't be this fookin' good.

But she knew that little voice was fooking wrong as soon as she saw the knife in the guy's hand. He was coming at her, baring his teeth, and somewhere in the distance she heard a woman shriek. The man was almost on her, and he was saying something—it sounded like *"she-devil."*

She managed to reach into her handbag, grab the gun. Before the guy could reach her she whipped the gun out and fired a shot, hitting him right in his goddamn face.

Then she ran, past the guy's idling car, trying to get to Rufus. She didn't make it. She had her hand on the door when she felt an intense pain ripping through her chest. The next moment she was on the ground, lying on her stomach with her cheek on the pavement. She saw a blurry image of a guy leaning out the open door of the idling car, holding a gun. It was Sebastian, that bastard.

Her last vision was of Sebastian, smiling, blowing spoke away from the barrel of the gun. She couldn't believe it. Of all the guys who could've done her in, it had to be that useless fookin' wuss? Talk about last laughs. That God, he had some fucking sense of humor.

Twenty

Sebastian was getting a tad cranky, just how long were
they going to follow this bloody car? They'd dropped
back when Yanni had realized they'd been spotted, but
then had caught up with Angela again a few miles further on, and as far as they could tell, no one in Angela's
car had noticed them since.

He had another shot of gin and realized he needed
a piss and bad. Paula, awake now in the back seat, was
scribbling notes—didn't that make her sick, writing in
a moving car like that? He hefted the Walther in his
hands and by golly it was true, the gun maketh the
man. That and a Savile Row suit, carnation in the but-
tonhole, of course. The car in front finally showed
brake lights and Yanni stopped, cut the engine. They
could see a trailer park, and Sebastian thought, A rather
shabby one, my dear.

Darkness was coming but they could see Angela,
the Fisher chappie, some brooding-looking white guy
in a combat jacket, and the mammoth black guy. Yanni
raised his gun and hissed, "Now you die, you whore."

Sebastian could hear Paula take a deep breath and he put his hand on Yanni's arm, a very risky gesture, and said, "Steady on, old bean, you do it now, it's too quick, she doesn't get to *feel* it—and most importantly we don't get any money."

Yanni withdrew the gun, muttering a string of obscenities. Sebastian could swear his own beloved Mummy was in there.

Paula said, "I didn't know there was going to be, like, you know, shooting and stuff."

Yanni turned to her, spat on the seat, said, "Shut your mouth, you harlot."

Sebastian thought that was more than a little rude and really, wasn't it crossing the line? He began to wonder if ol' Yanni had just the *tiniest* issue with women.

The trailer door opened and Angela and the black chappie came out, got in the car and took off.

Yanni, putting the car in gear, asked, "What is this?"

Paula said, "Probably going to get supplies. There's gotta be a 7-Eleven close by. You got a trailer park, you got a 7-Eleven."

Sure enough they pulled up outside said establishment and, lordy, was Angela *necking* with the black fellow?

Sebastian muttered, "Get a room. And herpes."

Finally, she got out and went into the store.

"Herpes," Paula said. "That's funny, Max was just telling me the story today, how Angela gave him herpes and how she said she got it from her ex-boyfriend, the Irish hit man."

Just what Sebastian needed to hear—the bloody history of his condition.

"I kill the she-devil right now," Yanni said, leaving the gun on the seat and pulling out a long-bladed knife he'd brought along.

"Let's be sensible, shall we?" Sebastian said. "I wouldn't mind doing away with the cow myself, but I don't think you want to be committing a murder on CCTV now, do you?"

Paula, from the back seat, said, "Wait, you guys aren't serious, are you? You're not really going through with this, right?"

Then Angela was leaving the store, smiling bliss-fully, carrying an overstuffed bag of junk food, and Yanni was out of the car, charging her like a madman.

Paula shrieked, "Oh my God!" and then Angela pulled out a gun and shot Yanni right in the face. Sebastian had to give the ol' gell credit, she had some tricks up her sleeve. Or, rather, in her purse.

But Sebastian couldn't let her get any ideas and try to shoot him as well, could he? Beating her to the shot, so to speak, he aimed the Walther and fired at her back as she passed, hitting her spot on. Not bad at all. Rather like shooting pheasants.

Sebastian was still feeling right proud of his accom-plishment when he remembered the black guy waiting in the car. He was going to walk over, do away with him as well, but, dammit, the car was already speeding out of the car park.

*

Watching Angela get killed had been sad and horri-
fying, of course, and the image of the puddle of blood
pooling around her on the asphalt would stay with her
forever, but Paula wouldn't have traded the experience for anything. What true crime author gets a
ringside seat for a homicide? A double homicide if you
included the crazed Greek. After *The Max* was written
and published and beloved by millions, the demand
would be huge for a book solely about Angela Petrakos.
She was the ultimate femme fatale—hey, that wouldn't
make a bad subtitle, got to write that down—and who
would be more qualified than Paula to tell her story?
The ideas were vivid, so fresh in Paula's head, she
started scribbling them down in her pad, afraid she'd
forget them.

She'd written maybe three pages when she snapped
out of her writer's high and realized she was in the
back seat of a car with Lee Child's homicidal half-
brother driving.

Suddenly terrified, Paula asked, "What're you going
to do to me?"

Sebastian said, "Nothing much. No offense, gell,
but I don't really fancy lesbians, I'm afraid. And least
when it's not a *ménage*."

He pulled over on to the shoulder, took all her cash
and jewelry, and ordered her to get out of the car. She
shut her eyes and cringed, afraid he'd shoot her, but
he just said, "*Ciao, mi amore*," and left her in the dust.

Twenty-One

*"Shit, he thought, as his eyes glazed over
and the roaring in his ears slowly receded.
I can't believe I'm dying in a goddamn trailer."*
MICHELLE GAGNON, *The Tunnels*

When Rufus returned alone, Max instinctively got his piece and put it in the waistband of his jeans, like the cool guys did in the movies. Rufus entered the trailer, fell to his knees, sobbing like a baby, and began to spill out a story of some white guy offing Angela.

Max felt his heart lurch, Angela gone? He couldn't fucking believe it.

He shouted at Rufus, "Yeah, and how come you're still alive? And where's her body—you just left her lying there? I treat you like my son and this is what I get?"

He had his gun in his hand and could feel grief and rage engulfing him.

Rufus was pleading and crying and then Max heard him say he loved her. *Loved* her? His Angela? And, worse, Rufus was going on now about how they'd been kissing just before she got wasted, how she was the best damn kisser he'd ever met. *It was so tender, yo, so sweet.*

Kissing?

He put the first round in Rufus's belly—weren't gut shots supposed to be agony? —and Rufus stared up at him with shock in his eyes. Max jammed the barrel in Rufus's mouth, went, "Fucking kiss this."

Emptied the clip.

Sean had been in a drunken stupor but the gunfire woke him—you want a mick's attention, let off a few rounds. He staggered out of the back room, the pump shotgun in his hands and saw the black man's almost headless torso lying at Max's feet.

Sean looked stunned, like he was in awe of Max, and why wouldn't he be? Guy from Ireland, IRA connections, he must've seen a lot of crazies in his bedraggled life, but there was crazy and there was Max crazy. Max knew he took insanity to a whole new level. Nobody was as crazy as he was, nobody.

Sean carefully lowered the shotgun, then asked, "W-w-w-w-w-w-w-where's A-A-A-A-A-Ang-g-g-g-gel-l-l-la?"

Max said, "She's dead. The love of my life, mon cherie, mon amour, mon Juliette."

Sean said, "Sh-sh-sh-she…w-w-w-w-was…m-m-m-m-mine."

"Well she's no one's now," Max said. "Saddle up pilgrim, time to hit the trail."

They packed fast and burned rubber out of there like the very Hound of Heaven was after them.

Max, sipping from the remains of the Jay while

Sean drove, began a long monologue about Angela and busts and dickless cracker kids. Then he punched Sean on the shoulder, a tear in his eye, and said, "Last of the *campaneros*."

Twenty-Two

"Words are not as adequate as teeth."
TOM PICCIRILLI, *The Dead Letters*

Paula Segal was stunned. She had written what she felt was a very compelling proposal for *The Max*, which included a synopsis of the entire book, and pretty soon expected to be living the literary high life—author tours, press conferences, award ceremonies. One thing she wasn't expecting—rejection.

Her agent broke the news to her over—yep—lattes at Starbucks.

He said, "There was a fairly strong consensus among the editors I went out to. The material's simply too dark."

Paula was in shock. This had to be a bad dream, or at least a bad joke. Her agent would crack a smile at any moment, say, Had you going there, huh? And then unveil the real news, that there was currently a bidding war going on for the book. All the major houses wanted it, and it was only a matter of whose eight-figure deal to accept: Knopf's or Harper Collins'. Or maybe there was only one major player, Sonny Mehta from Knopf, and on a signal from her agent Sonny would come through the door, ear-to-ear smile, and give her a big welcoming hug and say, "Welcome aboard, hon."

But, nope, her agent was still looking at her with that helpless expression that she'd gotten to know all too well over the years as her fiction-writing career had descended farther and farther into the toilet. But this wasn't fiction, this was non-fiction, true crime. This was supposed to be where all the bucks were, and she had the inside track on the hottest crime story of the year.

"What the hell do you mean, too dark? It's crime, it's murder, it's drugs, it's a riot, it's a prison break, it's IRA hit men, it's cold-blooded murder. It's *supposed* to be fucking dark."

Paula was yelling. A few customers and the baristas were looking over.

"Believe me, I understand where you're coming from." Her agent was looking around, smiling apologetically. "But there's dark and there's dark. As Ken Wishnia says, there're twenty-three shades of black."

She didn't want to hear about fucking Wishnia, she wanted to hear about a fucking book deal.

"Okay, so we got some rejections," she said. "Big whoopty shit. What's the next move?"

Her agent looked discouraged again, said, "Well, there's the second tier, but if I'm being completely honest I think it's unlikely the second tier will be interested. I went out with this fairly wide and, just to be completely up front, we didn't hear anything very encouraging from anybody. They all said the same thing: subject matter too dark, characters too unlikable."

"Wait," Paula said, knowing what was coming next. "What do you want me to do? You're saying you want me to—"

"How about writing a young adult novel?"

"You've gotta be kidding. You want me to give up *The Max*, my baby?"

"It's not a matter of what I want," he said. "It's what the market wants. And the market doesn't want Max Fisher."

"Bullshit," Paula said. "Bull fucking shit."

She stormed out of the Starbucks, deciding, Fuck agents, she'll sell it herself. How hard could it be to sell a hot property, the next *In Cold Blood*?

She sent the proposal out with a well-thought-out cover letter to practically every editor in New York and they all had the same response—story too dark, characters too unlikable. It had to be collusion, some kind of conspiracy. Or maybe her agent was bad-mouthing her all over town? Something like that. Years as a telemarketer had primed her well for rejection, but hearing all the negativity about *The Max* was tough to take. She was doubting herself, starting to lose hope.

She was almost ready to give up, head back to the call center, when she opened a copy of *Time Out New York* and saw that Laura—yes, *her* Laura—was reading tonight from her latest book at the Barnes & Noble on Union Square. She thought, *Has to be a sign*.

She rushed to her salon, demanded an appointment even though her hairdresser's schedule was full for the day. When Sergio asked her what she wanted done she took out a copy of *Mystery Scene* with Laura on the cover and said. "I want to look like *her*."

Sergio gave her the Lippman do, a short bob, flirty and sexy but not too showy about it. Afterward she couldn't have been more pleased. She looked as classy as Laura herself. When Laura saw her she'd have to realize they were meant to be together. Drinks would follow, maybe dinner, another meeting or two. Maybe she'd eventually move in with Laura in Baltimore, or they could just travel around the world together, two hot literary goddesses on the road...

And in the meantime Laura would help her get *The Max* into the hands of an editor who didn't have his head so far up his ass he couldn't see Pulitzer Prize material when it was handed to him.

A few minutes after Paula arrived at Barnes & Noble, Laura entered, rushing in, taking off her coat as she went, elegant and graceful as always, smiling, saying hello to all her adoring fans. Paula, in the front row, was staring at her, trying desperately to make eye contact. Surely Laura would remember her from the bar in El Paso and from their Internet exchanges. But after apologizing breathlessly for being late—traffic, her cab couldn't *budge*—and telling an effortlessly witty story about her signing the night before at the Mystery One bookstore in Milwaukee, Laura went right into her talk, and then read from her latest Tess Monaghan mystery. The book was another winner, no surprise there. A line of about thirty people formed, and Paula got on it at the end. Her heart was racing.

She was worried that she might actually pass out. How embarrassing would that be? Fainting at her future lover's book signing.

Finally it was Paula's turn. She handed over a copy of Laura's book and Laura, smiling, said, "Thank you so much for coming. Who should I make it out to?"

Paula thought, *It's not possible. She's looking right at me.*

Then she thought, Come on, cut the poor woman some slack. After all, she was a best-selling novelist in the midst of a major book tour. She was probably burnt out, that's all.

"You can make it out to me. Paula Segal."

Still no recognition.

"So how've you been?" Paula asked.

Now Laura looked at her, the first prolonged eye contact. She was squinting, trying to get it to click.

"You know, Paula Segal. We met at Left Coast Crime in El Paso a few years ago?"

Still nothing.

Trying to jar her memory, Paula said, "You know, Paula *Segal*. I was a Barry Award finalist. I write the McKenna Ford mysteries?"

After a few seconds Laura's face suddenly brightened and she said, "Oh, right. It's great seeing you again. How are you?"

"I'm fine, thank you."

Paula was trying to hold Laura's gaze, to let her know she was interested in a lot more than just getting a stupid book signed.

Then Laura said, "Should I make it out to you, McKenna?"

"No, my name's Paula."

"Oh, that's right, I'm sorry, Paula," Laura said. "It's been a crazy day. How do you spell your last name?"

"S-E-G-A-L."

Was it possible that Laura actually didn't remember her?

Nah, Laura had to remember.

"Yeah, so, I'm writing the Max Fisher story," Paula said. Then she couldn't help adding, "For Knopf."

Paula was proud of the way she'd just casually dropped that little lie, and prouder of how she'd been so modest about it. Like, Yeah, I've written the biggest true crime story of the new millennium, but it was no biggie, just another day in the life of a future Pulitzer winner.

Laura finished writing, handed her back the book, said, "I'm sorry, Fishman?"

"Fisher," Paula said. "You know, *Max Fisher*? The infamous businessman-slash-drug dealer who escaped from Attica last month?"

Laura looked lost then smiled and said, "I'm sorry, I've been touring for three weeks straight and I'm a little behind on the news lately. But that's great, congratulations. I wish you lots of luck with it."

The next guy in line was holding a stack of books and was inching closer. Laura was already smiling in his direction, making eye contact with him. But there was no way Paula was moving along—not yet anyway.

She didn't want to blow her one opportunity. After all, when would she get a chance like this again?

"I was thinking," Paula said, "maybe we could go out for a drink after you finish up here. You know, just to catch up."

"Oh, I'm sorry," Laura said. "I'd love to, really, but I have plans."

"Just one drink," Paula said.

Shit, was she being too insistent? No, just eager, that's all, and there was nothing wrong with eagerness. Eagerness was the way she'd made it as far as she had. If she weren't an eager beaver she never would've landed the Fisher project in the first place.

But did Laura just say "I can't"?

Nah, must've heard her wrong.

"So what time's good?" Paula asked. "Maybe around eight o'clock, eight thirty?"

"I said I can't make it."

Paula was stunned, went, "Please, it'll be so great. We have so much in common we can probably go on and on, talking all night long."

"I'm sorry, but I'm actually having dinner with Dennis Lehane tonight."

Den, it figured. Paula knew Lehane from the convention circuit. Nice guy, he'd bought her a couple of beers at Bouchercon in Chicago. For an hour she'd gushed to him about how much she loved *Mystic River* —the book, not the film—but did he ask for her room key or even her phone number? Um, no. God, Paula was so glad she was through with men. But there was no way Paula was going to let fucking Dennis Lehane or anyone else get in the way of her and Laura. She decided to take a chance.

"But I love you," she nearly shouted.

Paula knew she'd rushed it, that she should've at least waited till they'd had a chance to talk a little. But desperate times and all that.

Laura seemed totally confused and maybe a little shocked. She said, "I'm sorry?"

"I've known it since we met in El Paso, Laura. We're soul mates, we have everything in common, we should be spending the rest of our lives together."

A bookstore employee came over and said, "You're going to have to step away, ma'am. Other people want to get their books signed too."

How had this happened? How had it all gone to shit so quickly?

"We have to be together," Paula pleaded. "I've read *Charm City* twelve times. I nominate you for the Anthony every year. I even read your fucking short story in *Bloodlines.*"

"Ma'am," the bookstore employee said.

"Shut up, you skinny little bitch," Paula said.

Shit, did she really just say that? Why was Laura getting up, backing away? Why was someone yelling for security?

"Laura, wait, come back here!"

Paula tried to go after her but a security guard grabbed her and hauled her toward the escalator. Laura was receding into the distance and Paula found herself screaming, "We were meant to be together! You were going to give me a fucking blurb!"

But Paula couldn't even see Laura anymore.

"You're off my top friends on My Space, bitch!" she yelled, her voice carrying as she was led out to the shameful street.

Twenty-Three

"We would all end up in an explosion of colliding bodies,
clogging the cosmos with flying shit."
JIM THOMPSON, *Child of Rage*

Somewhere in North Dakota, Max and Sean crossed the border into Canada. Max didn't mind getting into the trunk, his only worry was that the dumb mick would forget to let him out.

Turned out his concerns were justified.

Over an hour after the border crossing Max was still screaming, banging, trying to get the fucker's attention. Good thing he had his piece with him and could shoot a couple of holes in the trunk or he would've suffocated. Still, for a while he thought he might die back there, trapped in a trunk. What a way to go. The gunfire had set up a whole range of odd sounds in his head and it was almost like music. He laughed out loud, thinking, *Now there's a title for a book, Trunk Music.*

See, The M.A.X. was always working the angles, never stopped with his sheer genius. You put some other bollix—and using the word, he shed yet again another tear for his beloved Angela—in the trunk of a car, he'd be screaming in panic. But The M.A.X., he was thinking up book titles.

Finally the idiot pulled over, opened the trunk, babbling, "S-s-s-s-s-s-sorry...M-M-M-Max. I fuh-fuh-fuh-fuh...gah-gah-gah..."

Max slapped him around a little, nothing too heavy. After all, he needed the kid, he was stupid but a good driver, another fucking Rain Man, and a big-time prison escapee like Max Fisher couldn't be driving himself around, now, could he? Yeah, the guy had been some kind of legendary paramilitary, but all the fight had gone out of him ever since Angela died.

It was starting to sink in for Max, just what he'd accomplished. He turned on the radio, listened to reports of the Attica riots on NPR as they drove. Forty-two people had been killed, including six guards and, of course, there was also Angela and Rufus and the crazy Greek, though the authorities hadn't put it all together yet. But who was left standing? That's right, the only legend in these here parts was The M.A.X.

And get this—the reports were calling him "armed and dangerous." Man, did that sound good! Meanwhile, he was a free man, in fucking Canada. It made Max want to weep. Maybe there was justice in the world after all.

Later, they stopped off at a shopping mall and Sean went to feed his face. There was a small bookstore and Max went in, looked at the bestsellers to see if *The Max* was number one yet. Nope. Zilch. Nada. The fuck was up with that? Some guy named Richard Aleas was selling well but no Paula Segal.

The clerk was eying him and Max, afraid he'd get recognized, figured he'd better buy something. He spotted the Will and Ian Ferguson book, *How To Be a Canadian*.

Bought that, the clerk asking, "On vacation?"

Max answered him in an Irish brogue, another little tribute to Angela, saying, "Ary, no, I'm over here to see me cousins."

Boy, he thought that was pitch perfect. The tiny germ of an idea was taking shape in his head.

While he was waiting for Sean to return he flicked through the book and found this:

> *There is nothing you can't discuss in Canada when it comes to sex. Do not talk about love, however. That makes Canadians uncomfortable.*

Then, from behind him he heard, "T-t-t-tis me."

Here was Sean, ketchup on his upper lip.

Max muttered, "Fuck on a bike."

Across the mall from them were two Mounties and, seeing them, Sean said, "Th-th-th-th-they…a-a-a-a-a-always……g-g-g-g-get…their m-m-m-m-man."

Max, trying out some more Irish, hissed, "Don't you be drawing bad luck down on us, laddie."

Then he thought, Wait, was that more like Scottish?

They got back in the car, more of fucking Canada. Was this country, like, endless? They were in the middle of nowhere and Max saw a sign saying *Grand Prairie, 479 Kilometers*. Gee, now that was something to look forward to, a grand prairie. Jesus Christ, a guy could get fucking bored in this place. Where were all the goddamn people?

Meanwhile, Sean—Jesus, Mary and Joseph, the guy was getting on Max's fucking nerves. The constant stuttering, not understanding a goddamn word he was saying. They checked into a motel and Sean in the bathroom started going, "T-t-t-t-t…f-f-f-f-f-f-fah…l-l-l-l-lo-lo-lah…" Max screamed, "The fuck're you saying? Lolita? What the fuck about Lolita?" and Sean continued, "L-l-l-l…g-g-g-g-g-g-ga…" Max didn't know if know if the guy had a speech impediment or he was just a fucking moron, but there was a limit to how much more of this shit he could take. He was a patient guy but this was fucking ridiculous.

The next day, they were driving, continuing north and west. They bought burgers and were eating them on the side of the road, and Sean started going, "You want some k-k-k-k-k-k-ketch-ketch-ketch," and Max suddenly lost it and said, "I'll give you ketchup, you stuttering fuck," and shot the asshole in the head, in mid-stammer.

Max shot him again, and that shut him up for good.

He took Sean's wallet and passport and then pushed him out of the car, onto the side of the road, where there was a bit of scrub to cover the body. Then he wiped up the car as much as he could using the paper napkins from the burgers and took off on his own.

He kept the radio turned off, didn't want to hear about *armed and dangerous* or *hot pursuit*. Man, it was nice to have Sean off the board. In the silence, though, he could hear Sean's voice, going, *Th-th-th-th-they…a-a-a-a-a-always……g-g-g-g-get…their m-m-m-m-man*, and he almost wished the fuck was still alive, just so he could shoot him again.

He wouldn't have thought it possible, but Canada was even more boring when you were driving through it all by yourself. He was missing Angela like hell. He knew it was crazy to miss a bitch who'd fucked up his life twice and probably would have fucked it up again, but he felt like he'd lost a, well, a part of himself. Things just wouldn't be the same without her around. Even when he was locked up in jail, thinking he'd never see her again, it was nice knowing she was out there somewhere.

In Edmonton, he checked into a hotel under Sean's name, using the cash from Sean's wallet to pay. But this couldn't go on for long. The money would run out and then what?

He was drinking again—what else was there to do in Canada? It was too goddamn *calm* here, everyone was too goddamn nice. He needed edge, he needed assholes, he needed America. Besides, he was certain that while he was up here freezing his nuts off he was missing out on all his fame back home. That dame's book was probably exploding right now, it was probably bigger than *Da Vinci* and *Potter,* and Scorcese was probably filming the movie, or maybe Spielberg. God, Max loved that. Spielberg knew how to yank the heartstrings and when Max got sent away to Attica the whole audience would be fucking bawling. If he was in New York right now he'd probably be mobbed by adoring fans, signing autographs. Instead he was holed up in a motel in Saskatchewan, or wherever the hell he was, living under the name Sean Mullan.

Then the idea hit him—a way to get back in the game, to get back on top. It was so obvious, he didn't know why he hadn't thought of it sooner.

A few days later, he drove to the Washington border, at the Pacific Crossing on Route 15. He did his DD of course, found out from some locals at the pub that the best time to cross the border was early morning, and that of all the border inspectors the young blond guy in the leftmost lane was the most lax. Max waited another couple of weeks for his beard to come in a little thicker, then he dyed it red.

The morning he was going to attempt to cross the border, Max checked himself out in the mirror, compared his appearance to Sean's passport photo. It wasn't too bad. Yeah, Max looked a lot older, but if Sean had put on some weight and started losing his hair since having the photo taken, it wasn't so far off.

All right, so maybe the resemblance wasn't there at all but, fuckit, Max had to give it a shot.

He drove to the border, stayed in the left lane. Sure enough, a young blond guy took his passport, asked, "Enjoy your time in Canada?"

"Yes, had me a great time," Max said.

Bingo, the brogue was working in full force. So far, so good.

The guy was looking at the passport, said, "I have an aunt from Ireland."

"Is that right, is it?" Max asked.

Who gave a fuck, but he had to keep the BS going.

"Yeah, from Limerick. That near where you're from?"

"No, me from Belfast," Max said.

Shit, that sounded more Tarzan than Irish. At least the lilt was okay. He had to stay with it.

"Oh, yeah?" the guy said. "It's rough over there, I imagine. Bombs going off all the time, right?"

Would the asshole let him through already?

"Oh, a few wee bombs," Max said. " 'Tis nothing."

The guy squinted, "You got anything on you? Any weapons?"

Max had unloaded all the hardware. Only had one piece, a SIG, tucked away just in case.

"No, no weapons, me afraid. Me left me weapons back in Belfast."

The guy looked at Max closely, squinted, said, "Why do I feel like I've seen you before?"

"Maybe 'tis an Irish thing," Max said. "Don't the Brits say we all look alike?"

He thought this would at least get a laugh.

"No, that's not it," the guy said. "You come through here before?"

Max, sweating through his shirt, said, "Sometimes. I have me family in Seattle and I visit them every wee while."

Fuck, he was losing it. The whole plan was going to shite.

"Irish family in Seattle, huh? How'd they wind up there?"

Max couldn't think of anything, said, "Gold rush."

"Gold rush?"

"Yes, 'tis an old wing of me family. 'Tis a rich wing, too."

"I thought the gold rush was California?"

"Aye, 'tis true, but they weren't the smartest people, me relatives."

The guy squinted at Max again, as if studying him, then smiled and said, "Well, welcome to America, Mr. Mullan. It's a pleasure to have you back."

Driving away slowly Max could barely contain himself. He was back on his home turf—America, the land of freedom. Yeah, okay, there was a downside, he had to be fucking Irish, maybe for the rest of his life, but hey, he could pull it off. After all, how hard could it be to be Irish? He already liked to drink and kill people, he'd be a goddamn natural.

Humming that anthem Angela used to sing, *The Soldier's Song*, he drove at a nice easy pace till he hit the open road. Then, thinking he better start getting used to his new identity, he shouted "Bollix to ye all!" and fucking floored it.

THE
END

Get Hard Case Crime by Mail...
And Save 43%!

☐ **YES! Sign me up for the Hard Case Crime Book Club!**

As long as I choose to stay in the club, I will receive every Hard Case Crime book as it is published (generally one each month). I'll get to preview each title for 10 days. If I decide to keep it, I will pay only $3.99* — a savings of 43% off the cover price! There is no minimum number of books I must buy and I may cancel my membership at any time.

Name: _____

Address: _____

City / State / ZIP: _____

Telephone: _____

E-Mail: _____

☐ **I want to pay by credit card:** ☐ VISA ☐ MasterCard ☐ Discover

Card #: _____ Exp. date: _____

Signature: _____

Mail this page to:
HARD CASE CRIME BOOK CLUB
20 Academy Street, Norwalk, CT 06850-4032

Or fax it to 610-995-9274.
You can also sign up online at www.dorchesterpub.com.

* Plus $2.00 for shipping. Offer open to residents of the U.S. and Canada only. Canadian residents please call 1-800-481-9191 for pricing information.

If you are under 18, a parent or guardian must sign. Terms, prices, and conditions subject to change. Subscription subject to acceptance. Dorchester Publishing reserves the right to reject any order or cancel any subscription.